IF HOME
WAS A PERSON

IF HOME
WAS A PERSON

AN AFRICAN + AMERICAN ROMANCE NOVEL

by

R Fennell & E Moyo

If Home Was a Person
R Fennell & E Moyo

Paperback ISBN: 979-8-88796-972-5
Ebook ISBN: 979-8-88796-973-2

Contents

Chapter One

INTRODUCTION

The blue sky is as vast as the eye could see, embracing the sun that nestled within. The camera swoops in at that moment, zeroing on a particular person. On a busy street, packed with other humans, the simmering attraction of this particular woman set her apart from the rest. She radiated a magnetism that drew people's attention to her. But thirty-three year old Tapiwa was oblivious to their stares. Her attention was on a different matter altogether. She found herself squinting against the glare of the sun, a reminder that time was constantly ticking. "I better get going." She muttered.

As she turned towards the opposite direction, the clickety-clack of her red heels filled the air, striking confidently against the concrete surface. She moved with a purpose, her heart beating steadily. Turning left once more, she walked to the front of a white washed building, the sign *"Jeran."* boldly written on its sign. "Here goes nothing." She whispered beneath her breath, pushing the glass door open. The moment she walked in, she could feel the change in temperature. Gone was the stinging feeling of the burning sun, and in place was a cool ambience. Tapiwa walked to the receptionist, and said. "Hi, I have an appointment with Ms. Lyra for 10:30 am."

"Hello, welcome to Jeran. Just one minute." The receptionist replied, checking through the log showing on the computer's screen. "Right on time." She confirmed. "You can go upstairs. It is the first room to the left." The woman directed.

"Alright thanks." Tapiwa replied, moving forward. She began to wonder what was up with lefts today. "Everything seems to be going left, I hope it is a good sign." She thought. Knocking softly, she paused for a moment, before pushing the door open.

A caramel-skinned lady, who was probably in her fifties stood up from behind her desk. "Hi, you are here." The woman greeted, stretching her hand out for Tapiwa.

"Yes, it's nice to meet you." Tapiwa replied, her lips stretching into a smile.

"Thank you for sparing time for this interview."

"Nah, it's okay. I really look forward to it to." Tapiwa assured, taking off her outer coat.

"Please have a seat." The woman said, pointing to the other chair.

"Yeah, thanks." Tapiwa replied. For the first time since she appeared in the building, she felt somewhat nervous. She wondered how and when the interview would start. "So…" She began, trailing off.

"Right. You've been briefed by Nichole, I hope?" The woman asked.

"Kind of." Tapiwa shrugged.

"Well, it's not a problem. I can go over it all. You will be asked some questions regarding your personal history, and the book you are currently writing. The interview is to take place for three days. I hope you're prepared for that?" The woman asked.

"Yes, I-

"You can call me Lyra." The woman cut in.

"Yes, I am prepared for that Lyra." She said.

"Well, well. We are starting somewhere." Lyra said, standing up once more. "We should move to the studio." She said.

"Ah, yes." Tapiwa replied, also standing. She picked up her coat, folding it across her left arm.

"This way, please." Lyra said, stepping out of the room. Tapiwa followed in silence, and once more, the corridor of the building echoed the sound of her clicking heels. At the very end of the hall, Lyra pushed open a door, and it was almost like Tapiwa had stepped into another world. Despite how silent it was outside, the inside was anything but that. Loud music blared, flashing lights filled the air, and the feeling was very much different.

"Leto, I am here." Lyra yelled out. Few seconds passed by, before a young man appeared.

"Lyra!" He greeted with the familiarity associated with a close friend. "And this is –" He trailed off, setting his gaze on Tapiwa.

"Tapiwa." Tapiwa said, filling in the blank.

"Oh, such a unique name." The young man said, tilting his head to the left. "I am Leto." He said. His expression changed as a sudden realization cut across his face. "Oh, the author, it's a pleasure meeting you." He said, stretching his hand out.

"Likewise." Tapiwa responded, shaking his hand.

"Are we on time?" Lyra asked, directing her word to Leto.

"Just a moment." He said, and then he was gone again. A split second later, he was back. "Okay, we are ready." He said. He led them to a back room, much calmer, with a lot of equipment Tapiwa had not seen before. She observed with a calm awe. Although her expression remained the same, she soaked in all the details her eyes came across.

For the next few hours, Tapiwa was the main character in the whole room. They made her hair, her makeup, and set up the equipment they were about to use. As she stared at the camera, her pupils dilated, and she wondered if she would do well. She began to think of all the moments that led up to this – of all the times she had to try something new.

"Are you ready ma'am?" The cameraman asked.

"Ye- yeah." She responded, clearing her throat. "I am ready." She said.

4

"One, two, action!"

"Good morning, welcome to your number one TV station news and updates. I am your host Lyra McKinnon, taking you through this session. Our guest today is Ms. Tapiwa Moyo, who is the co-author of the popular novel – Black Romance. Thank you for gracing us with your presence." Lyra said.

"Thank you for having me over." Tapiwa said, forcing a stiff smile. She winced inwardly, wondering if her expression was the right one.

"Can you briefly introduce yourself to the audience?" Lyra asked.

"My name is Tapiwa, and I am the co-writer of the novel Black Romance."

"We learnt that you were originally from Zimbabwe?" Lyra queried.

"Yes, I came from a city called Harare; which means the city that doesn't sleep. You can think of it as a small version of New York."

"Harare, that's amazing. I have never been there, but it is famously known for its beautiful jacaranda-lined streets."

"That is correct." Tapiwa responded, the tension slowly easing from her body. Talking about somewhere she had come from had that effect, she guessed.

"Can you tell us a bit about your background, and what led to you migrating to Canada?" Lyra asked.

"I grew up in a Christian home. The expectations were to finish school, get a degree, get married and have children. But then, I moved to Canada at the tender age of nineteen all by myself after high school. Economically it was a good move, but I found myself alone most of the time."

"Oh my, that must have been scary. I can't imagine myself moving across the world, by myself to start a new life." Lyra said. "How did you cope?"

"I would be lying if I said my life was smooth sailing, or if everything was terrible. My life was a mixture of both…" Tapiwa shrugged. "Looking back to those moments that seem impossible, I realized that every little thing happened for a reason. Now at thirty-three, life has shown me so many lessons."

"That's incredible Tapiwa. Before we divulge into the book, there is a part I want to ask about. So you travelled to Tulum for a reason, but left a different person. Can you explain or tell a sneak peak about what you mean?" Lyra asked.

"Travel is my therapy and escape. Little did I know that I would find love in Tulum." Tapiwa said shyly, before looking back up. She turned towards the camera, grinning from ear-to-ear as she said "I hope every reader enjoys this book, and understands the synergy between the two writers."

Chapter Two

THE STARS ALIGNED

The interview was progressing smoothly, and Tapiwa didn't feel the invisible pressure she had felt earlier. Although the flashing lights were forever constant, she had slowly adjusted to the instant exposure.

"So we will move on to the first chapter of the book." Lyra said. "Is that okay with you?"

"It's all good, no problem." She replied. With a nod, she began. "Chapter one." Tapiwa said. The pages of the book flipped to the past, and Tapiwa found herself thrust to the time she had once witnessed.

A year ago

Tulum was always on the top of Tapiwa's travel lists. But she was always hesitant to travel alone. It also didn't help that she had heard many horror stories about tourist killings in Mexico. But curiosity was a sweet poison that entangled its prey. It kept strangling, pulling its prey deeper into the pool of wonder. Tapiwa became intrigued by pictures and videos she had seen on social media. And little by little, the pool of curiosity had expanded into a sea. But as usual, life has a way of throwing in its little quirks – an oddity, a situation, a moment. At this time, traveling outside the country had been restricted for the past two years, but as fate would have it - the restrictions were finally been lifted. Excited, exhilarating and at the same time Tapiwa was scared. She was terrified of being stuck in another country with COVID, and having to pay ridiculous amounts of money to quarantine.

A myriad of emotions began to run through her mind, doubts tainting the decision she had once made. Groaning, she twisted her head to the side, looking out the window. Although the curtains were down, from the far corner she could see outside a bit. There was nothing but darkness, and the sight did nothing to calm her raging thoughts. Rolling onto her back, she stared at the ceiling for a few more seconds, taking it all in. "Should I just travel to Jamaica?" She whispered to herself. It was relatively safer compared to going to Mexico, right? She wondered. But once again, fate was at its play. The sound of her phone ringing broke into her thoughts, causing her to groan once more. She thought of ignoring it, but the persistent tone wouldn't go away. "Ugh, this better be good." She grumbled, scrambling out of bed. As her feet connected with the soft rug next to her bed, her toes curled from the ticklish contact.

As she glanced at the screen, the name 'Krystal' was displayed proudly. It was one of her closest friend. Tapiwa swallowed the complaints deep in her throat, swiping the accept button.

"Hey girl." She greeted.

"Girl, where did you keep your phone? I have been calling like forever."

"I was about to sleep." Tapiwa said, sighing.

"Well, that aside, so-" Krystal paused, building the anticipation of that moment.

"So what?" Tapiwa queried.

"I am traveling baby." Krystal giggled, her excitement very much evident.

"Where?" Tapiwa asked, walking back to the bed. She sat down by the edge, adjusting the way she held the phone. "What did you say?" She asked, missing the last word Krystal had said.

"I said I am travelling to Mexico. I am going to Tulum." She chortled.

"Tulum?" Tapiwa repeated, feeling her heart bang as she heard the name. *'What the...'* she thought.

"Hey, are you still there?" The voice of her friend broke the fog in her mind.

"Yeah, yeah... I am." She rushed out. It was such a coincidence, and Tapiwa couldn't help but think this was a sign. There was only one thing that was left. "I guess two people are heading to Tulum." She said in a sing-song voice.

"Wait – what?" Krystal shrieked. "You going?"

"I guess I am." Tapiwa chuckled.

Tapiwa immediately changed her plans to go to Tulum. After all, time was constantly ticking, and there was no time to waste time. She got her ticket last minute, and although it was more expensive than the normal fare - Tapiwa did not care. She wasn't sure why or what force was driving her spontaneous-ity. But she gave in to the moment- relieving the feeling of shedding ones burden. She wanted to get away. She could not remember the last time she heard the sounds of the ocean.

Tapiwa had once read that people who have a connection to nature, according to scientific studies, are happier and healthier than those who do not. The mind, thought processes and emotions can all benefit from exposure to open skies and the blue highs. Spending time by the water, in particular, appears to be fundamentally satisfying for her; releasing a flood of soothing hormones such as cortisol, catecholamine, and adrenaline. As a result, the stress levels in her body are reduced; including the development of her imagination, empathy, and perseverance. Tapiwa also noticed how easy it was to forget about her worries while surrounded by uncontaminated air, and the salty flavor of the sea.

She couldn't wait.

***

Getting to Mexico was just over five hours direct from Edmonton. This was at the end of April. For the rest of the world, winter was long gone. But for Alberta – the fog from winter had yet to be cleared. It had been a long winter.

Tapiwa did not think she would make it for her trip, because her passport was taking longer than usual to process. She was on the verge of canceling, but life had its own plans once again. When she got home two days before departure, her passport was ready. There was nothing to hold her back. Unfortunately, Tapiwa did not have much time to shop, but was sure to fill her bag with bottled water. She had once heard that the water in Mexico was bad, and would give one a stomach ache. Although she could not verify such claims, since she had never been there – she figured there was no point taking chances. The thought of falling sick during a vacation, was nothing short but a nightmare.

Cancun had an amazing view at landing. The airport was empty and enormous, but the exhilarating feeling she felt in her belly didn't diminish at all. She could feel her heart rate increase, her mouth run dry, and her palms palpitate for what was to come. As soon as she walked out of the airport door, she spotted different taxi drivers, competing for her attention. There were also car rental companies, boasting of the best prices and bargains. Tapiwa couldn't help but smirk as this reminded her of Harare; the hustle was real.

On a random, she decided to take a taxi to the resort she had booked a room. It was only the beginning of what was to come. Rolling the windows down, the wind accompanied the ride and she was able to see things beyond the confines of the car. Albeit short, it was enough for her heart to swell in a free will she had denied herself for so long. The charming city of Tulum looked like an image straight out of a postcard; bounded by azure Caribbean waters, and perfect beaches. The ride was all too short, and Tapiwa couldn't help but sigh in disappointment as the car slowed down in front of the resort she had booked a few days earlier.

"Thank you…" She called out, closing the door behind her with a thud. "This is it…" I muttered, heading inside. Tapiwa felt a bit nervous since she was all alone. Krystal and her friends wouldn't be around until three days later. She felt safer that way. The resort was exceptional, especially the service. It had a private beach, many pools and Jacuzzis. It was certainly the rest she needed. For the next few days, Tapiwa spent most of her time at the beach. It was family oriented, and she couldn't help but feel left out. The distant sound of people playing was carried by the wind; a familiar and serene moment. And being an introvert did not help. Tapiwa was left to herself. The food was also all inclusive, and after two days, she found herself sick of the buffet. She was glad to leave after three days.

Downtown Tulum was about forty minutes from the resort. Finding the boutique hotel was difficult and her cab driver was getting impatient. After a few attempts circling around the city, she found the small boutique hotel. It was the same as the pictures she had seen on a Google street map.

Looking back to those moments, Tapiwa could say that Tulum was a very simple city, with many restaurants and private beach clubs. It was nothing like the stereotypical image the outside world painted of Mexico. The locals were very friendly, and Tapiwa was able to experience the difference in culture. It was all new and refreshing, a side of the world she had never experienced. She was glad to be downtown. It had a much different vibe as compared to the resort. The resort was very modern, and she could not get around some amenities. For example, if she did not place her room card in a slot near the door, the electricity would not work. Tapiwa was puzzled by such tactics, but at the same time – impressed. The best feature of the room was the swinging bed.

Canada's climate was much different to Mexico, and Tapiwa felt the change. She could feel a sweat roll down her back, sticking the material of her dress to her skin. She eventually decided to go for a swim, and then grab a bite. As time slowly passed by, Tapiwa decided to go out. She decided to tour the heart of the city. She was in awe seeing many black people. It wasn't the color, but how a place of a different race and culture embraced people of other race and culture. The majority looked Black American. She would stop to admire couples walking down the street in nice outfits, holding hands and creating core memories. Eventually, she finally found a burger place. Tapiwa could not help but sit down all day just watching people pass by. Back in Canada, she lived in the countryside of Alberta, where there are only a handful of black people. At that moment, she felt she had made the right choice and it would only get better when she linked up with her friend, Krystal.

Krystal could be considered a social butterfly. She found all the events. She is a type of person that thrives of the energy of the people and things around her. Tapiwa was suddenly overcome with the urge to discover a gem before her friend came. The thought of such promise got Tapiwa on the move once more. She decided to walk to a bar called Mistico, as she was falling asleep with the heat. Mistico had a tropical design. And Tapiwa decided to stay for a little while. She decided to sit and enjoy the music. "I will be back." She muttered, got up and left.

Krystal and her friends arrived the next day, and true to her word –Tapiwa took them to the bar she had found.

"How did you find this place?" Krystal asked, more surprised than shocked

"I stumbled upon it." Tapiwa responded, shrugging. The feeling of spending time with friends was a different vibe entirely. She felt happier, laughed more, and couldn't wait to create more memories with them. They enjoyed the music, danced, and drank. It was a girl's trip that was already at its peak – or so she thought. But as she always knew, life always had different plans. And life's plan brought a man she had never met.

Chapter Three

FATE

Life brought Nate.

With the ambience of a thriving club; loud music, laughter, conversations and alcohol – it was the perfect club scene. Although Tapiwa wasn't big on clubs, she referred to that moment as normal more than pandemoniac fun. It was loud and pure chaos, but at the same time she was having fun. As Tapiwa soaked in that moment, her attention was focused on the different strangers all pooled in one place. The sound of laughter drew her attention back to the table with her friends. The strange man was having a conversation with Krystal, and whatever he was saying was funny enough for her to laugh. Tapiwa could not hear what they were saying above the loud music, but just as she was about to turn away, she heard the man say. *"I am here looking for my wife".*

Tapiwa was sure they had said a lot from the moment she wasn't paying attention. But then – she had heard that sentence clearly. Curiosity began to blossom in her mind. She watched as Krystal pointed towards her direction, followed by the gaze of the man that had caught her attention. She heard him utter something else, followed by a boisterous laughter from Krystal once more.

And then – he was here.

He was right in front of her, scooting next to the seat beside hers. She was startled, but at the same time she could see clearly the features she hadn't seen the first time. The man was tall and handsome, with chocolate skin as smooth like butter.

"Hi." He greeted, moving his lips closer to the direction of her ear, so she could hear his words.

"Hi." Tapiwa replied shyly, hoping he didn't notice how shy she was.

"I am Nate." He introduced. Tapiwa could finally place a name to the face. 'It suits him.' She thought, and she couldn't help but be shocked at her own thoughts.

"I came here to celebrate my birthday." He said, and Tapiwa couldn't help but stare intently at his face. Her heart rate began to increase little by little, her pulse skittering as she wondered what to say next.

"Do you want to guess what age I just turned?" He asked.

"Thirty-five?" She said.

"No."

"Thirty- eight?" She said, trying once more.

"I am flattered, but I am actually forty-five. I just turned forty-five." He said, his lip drawing into a slow smile. Tapiwa couldn't help but think he looked amazing, and much younger.

"You look so much younger." She said. "You should probably share your skin care routine." His smile turned into a rich chuckle, and Tapiwa could feel the nervous pit-a-pat form in her lower belly. She could not help but laugh too, and she realized that she had not once felt awkward with the stranger she had just met. "Have you ever been married?" She asked; a question from her intrusive thoughts.

Tapiwa winced inwardly, wondering if she had asked a question that was too personal. She was about to change topics, when he said. "No, I have never been married." Perhaps it was the smoke in the air, or the alcohol in her system, Tapiwa felt an edge she knew would be gone by morning's light. "How come you have never been married?" She queried, tilting her head to the right. "You must be problem." She stated. Her words sounded insensitive, but deep down Tapiwa was only curious. She wasn't persecuting him for his choices, but then again – she wondered *why?* "From where I come from, men marry by late twenties, anything beyond that age we view them as men who nag and cannot stay with a woman." She said.

"Well, it is the opposite in my place. Where are you from?" He asked.

"Zimbabwe." Tapiwa replied.

"I am from America, and you know, it's not that I haven't been in a relationship. I've been in long term relationships. We just haven't gotten to the point of marriage, because that's not an emphasis in America."

He explained, shrugging. "Most people just shack up in America. Well, most black folks." He said.

"So what was your longest relationship?" She asked him.

"That would be my daughter's mother. It lasted for fifteen years. So I guess you can consider that to be a marriage." Tapiwa couldn't help but laugh at his reply. It wasn't what she was expecting, but at the same time – it sounded so honest.

"Have you ever been married?" He asked.

"Yeah... I was married. But I am separated now, and I also have a daughter." Tapiwa replied. "She is four years old." She said proudly

As the night thinned out, Tapiwa found herself chattering away with a stranger she had only met. But then again, every introvert had a limit. Her social battery was completely exhausted, and she was ready to go back to the hotel. As she searched for her card to pay her bill, Nate swiped his card. It was such a kind gesture she did not expect.

"Do you want me to call a cab for you?" He asked.

"Oh no, don't worry. My hotel is within walking distance." Tapiwa replied.

"Alright, then I will walk you back to your hotel." He said. Tapiwa paused, thinking about it for a split second. Although she was exhausted, the edge was still very much present. In the end, she agreed to let him walk her back. On the way to the hotel, they started talking about future plans they had.

"I am sure Krystal and my other friends would rather go partying. But I am not much of the partying type." She shrugged. "I would rather go sightseeing." She said

"I want to go sightseeing myself." Nate said, stopping. "Would you like to go with me tomorrow?" He asked.

"Sure, it should be fun." Tapiwa agreed. As she looked up, she realized they were now in front of her boutique hotel. "I guess this is goodnight." She said.

"Yeah… Good night, I had a lot of fun." Nate responded, and at that moment they exchanged numbers.

***

Morning came soon enough, and the sun shined brightly up above; streaming through the window of the hotel room. Tapiwa groaned as a square of sun hit her in the eye, and slowly she woke up bit by bit; until finally, her eyes were wide open. Blinking rapidly, memories of yesterday came floating through, and she realized why the ceiling above felt so unfamiliar. "Hmm… *I am in Tulum. Tulum Mexico… I left the resort,*" Those thoughts floated through her mind. Staring at the ceiling blankly, Tapiwa slowly slipped back into oblivion before her mind caught up with her, and dragged her back to the present. Groaning, she twisted her head to the side, looking out the window. The glare of the sun made her squint; stealing the remnant sleep that was left behind. Rolling onto her back, she stared at the ceiling for a few more seconds, taking it all in. A content grin cut across her lips as she stretched her hands above her head; straightening out the kinks and twists in her joints. It felt like heaven, and she knew she wouldn't mind staying longer in bed.

But the sleep was gone, and left in place was building anticipation on how to plan her day. Scooting off the mattress, her feet connected with the soft rug spread out on the floor, and the pressure she once exerted on the bed was gone; in its place was an imprint – an imprint of her body. After an hour of self-care and revitalization, Tapiwa was looking forward to visiting the ruins. She was happy to see Nate's text. In the end, she decided to walk to his hotel as he had to switch rooms. She thought it would be nice to see a different hotel, and also help him move. He appreciated it.

Krystal and her friends were planning to spend the day at a beach club. Tapiwa decided to see the Tulum Ruins, and later on – join them. Although Tapiwa didn't mind spending time in their company; after all, she had fun. But in the end, their priorities were much different. There was a significant age gap between Tapiwa, Krystal and her friends. Her priority was sightseeing and excursions, but they were more into partying. She had been there.

The Tulum ruins are located on the eastern side of the Yucatan Peninsula, in Quintana Roo. The ruins are in the heart of the Rivera Maya on the Caribbean Sea. The sight was one Tapiwa would never forget. The numerous structures remained, spread out over groomed lawns and Oceanside cliffs. The site's buildings were an evolution of architectural styles that showcased the growth of the area over the centuries. It was a way for Tapiwa to dive into the rich Mexican culture and Mayan history.

Although Tapiwa had so much fun, communication was a challenge. She was constantly on the lookout for WIFI everywhere she went. But through it all, she was glad she had met someone who had similar interests, and also they could be each other's photographers. Tapiwa knew that if she was to plan a honeymoon, it would be exactly how she spent time with Nate for the rest of her trip in Tulum. Every moment was perfect; it felt like a dream. They discussed the past, the future and the present. He learned new things about her, and she learned new things about him. They were all core memories, and Tapiwa knew she would remember for as long as she lived.

They found a beach club, and had a couple's massage by the beach. They also went for a boat cruise, and Tapiwa couldn't resist the urge to record him snorkeling for the first time. She felt so comfortable around him, and she realized she could be her natural self without trying too hard. At the end of the day, they had dinner at an Italian restaurant. At that moment, with just the two of them – the soulful sound of Grover Washington started playing. It couldn't have been more perfect.

With a promise to keep, Tapiwa and Nate later went to a different restaurant where they met Krystal and her friends. Another guy from Miami was with them, and Tapiwa wanted to show Nate her swinging bed. He came up to her room, and Tapiwa was clear about one thing – although the moment they had was great, she told him they could not be intimate. They had their first kiss, and cuddled for the rest of the night. Although the day was devoid of bodily pleasures, the moment they shared was absolutely perfect. It was much more than the connection of carnal desires. It was a connection that tugged at their soul strings.

In the end, Tapiwa stayed with Nate until she left Tulum. There is a saying that goes – *If home is a person*. Nate felt like home, it was as if they had known each other for a lifetime. Tapiwa could imagine telling her friends about the moments they shared, and them thinking it was too good to be true. They had not a single moment of conflict, or the moment of awkwardness.

Tapiwa thought of extending her ticket, but it was too expensive. They spent the last night having dinner at a Mediterranean restaurant and a club called Horus. The last stop was where they first met - Mistico. The next day they had breakfast and a massage. They gave each other a deep hug, a kiss and said their goodbyes. Their moments felt like a novel... a movie romance that life had seen too many times. But to Tapiwa, it was special.

As she slowly walked down the boarding pass, there was one sentence that kept tingling in her mind. 'I can't wait to see him again'. It was a sentence that showed her deepest and most heartfelt desire.

Many questions ran through her head. *Was it too fast? Was it just being in a nice place and maybe it was just a temporary thing?* Tapiwa found herself caring for Nate, and kept in touch for over a month, but later on she flew to Atlanta to see him.

Chapter Four

LOVE DYNAMICS

Tapiwa pulled the ends of her coat closer, snuggling deeper into its warmth. The interview had ended a few minutes ago, and she was now on her way back home. It felt like she was in a daze, but as the harsh wind brushed against her face, she slowly came back to reality. "That went well." She muttered. She looked down at her red heels, a smile cutting across her lips. She had so many lefts today, but she guessed it was a sign for something good. "I miss him." She sighed, looking back up. An uber slowed down in front of where she stood. Tapiwa watched as the driver rolled down the window, poking his head out. "Ms. Tapiwa?" He called out.

"Yes. That's me." She responded. Taking a picture of the car, the license plate and the driver, Tapiwa finally got in. Although it was an awkward moment, Tapiwa knew she could never be too careful. As soon as the car began to move, she leaned backward, resting her head against the head rest. Rolling the window down, the wind slapped against her face, causing her nose and cheeks to sting. Different thoughts began to float through her mind, and slowly her mind focused on one.

Love.

It is an intricate thing; a myriad of emotions, behaviors, and beliefs related to strong feelings of affection, protectiveness, warmth, and respect for another person. It is an emotion that came in all forms. It could refer to non-human things, animals, principles, or a moment. While most people agree that love implies strong feelings of affection, there are numerous disagreements about its precise meaning, and one person's "I love you" may mean something entirely different to another. For example, love could be that of a mother, or from the love of a spouse, which differs from the love for food. But for Tapiwa, the love she felt for Nate was more than what three words could describe. It was more of a connection that went deeper than the shackles earth describes as love.

The love she felt encompassed a range of strong and positive emotional and mental states; from the most transcendent virtue or good habit, the deepest interpersonal affection, to the simplest pleasure.

Later on in life, Tapiwa realized that love is not enough. It forms the foundation, yes, but many factors contribute to a successful healthy relationship. Back in Zimbabwe, a man is regarded as the head of the household and the provider. Women are taught to be submissive to their husbands. But as the world was continually evolving, the roles slowly began to change. When she was growing up, Tapiwa witnessed such change as women started shifting their roles from being housewives to career women.

Tapiwa applauded her mother for giving up her career to raise her siblings and her. She remembered the day her mother left her job. She remembers such memories with a stark clarity. Her mother was working for a distribution company, and dedicated all her time and hard work to bring in an extra income. On her lunch breaks, she would pick them up from school, and then rush back to work. She would also work on the weekends, or stay late if there was a problem with trucks and orders.

When Tapiwa was in the fifth grade, she remembered staying late in the library, losing track of time. Tapiwa could still remember the fear she felt as she faced her furious mom. It was as cold as Antarctica, and as silent as a grave. As they drove broke home, the strings of fate pulled a terrible card on them. Her mother's car collided with a cyclist; the force of his body hitting the windshield sent him flying up in the air. Tapiwa could remember screaming, her mind clouded with terror as blood, glass shards and the seat belt bite into her skin. Tapiwa had never seen anyone flip in the sky so high. She remembers turning side ways to stare at her mother, whose face was a pale and white as a sheet of paper.

After that incident, her mother felt so bad she would often cry. A nightmare they had both lived through. Her parents had then decided that her mother should take a break, and raise the children, while her father made the money. There was no problem with such arrangement since her father made enough money. But her mom was an icon of resilience and perseverance. She didn't stop fighting, and found ways of making money whilst at home.

Tapiwa was opportune to see the difference in lifestyle. Although life was evolving, so many people remained stuck in their own ways. Women raised to expect the man to be the breadwinner, found it hard to live a different way. But with the economic situation fast changing, these expectations were no longer valid. And women on such track-line suffered the most. Men would rather marry educated women who will help with the bills. Tapiwa often thought about this question – if something happened to the sole breadwinner, *what happens to the family left behind? Where would such women start from? How would they survive? How would they cope with the harsh world?* She thought about it over and over again.

Tapiwa also had the opportunity to learn and observe the actions of her paternal grandmother. Her paternal grandfather passed away when her father was in primary school. He was a teacher, and then his health took a dive, and he went blind. Tapiwa's grandmother had to go above, and beyond to provide for her six children. She would make African beer that is referred to as maheu. And when that wasn't enough, she would farm. The tales her aunties told were one Tapiwa viewed with awe. They had to wake up at four in the morning to farm, and then go to school, and still work after they came back. By the time they were in class, they were so tired. And with so many admirable role models around, Tapiwa had these morals instilled to the very core of her being. She aimed higher, she worked harder.

Tapiwa believes that all humans go through different types of love throughout their lives, and expectations. In high school love is referred to as "puppy love". This is the first love humans' experience. It happens early in life, as early as primary school. It is innocent, pure, and sweet and an awakening to a myriad of emotions. It is a moment when we like the other person, spend time with them, and are attracted to them.

In primary school, Tapiwa was a nerd. She would spend most of her time reading books. But High School was the total opposite. She was regarded as the 'it' girl. Many guys, most especially her seniors, would profess their love to her; it went as far as the head boy. As she bloomed through puberty, her curves more prominent, and her beauty shining through the cracks of such age -Tapiwa enjoyed more attention, and found it difficult to like one person. She had one relationship in high school that was short lived. His name was Michael. . In high school everyone wants to be with the most popular guy, the all-rounder athlete, the most handsome, talented, bad guy and the rich kid. Michael had the talent and was popular. He was a really good dancer; he ended up going overseas and pursued his dancing career. He was a year younger than she was. Tapiwa remembered hanging out during sports events, and dance competitions.

He told Tapiwa, he would love to lose his virginity to her, which she declined; as she was scared at that time. Teenage couples often have people tell them that young love rarely lasts. These people aren't trying to be mean; they are trying to save teenagers from heartache. Chances are these people had their hearts broken by young love in the past, and are trying to spare the feelings of the teenager they are talking to. But every teenager has the same response to this – "it's going to be different for us. Eventually, she broke up with him.

Relationships are confusing for young people because they are experiencing feelings of romantic love and attraction for the first time. They are just starting to figure it all out. Since these are feelings that many mature adults struggle with, you can only imagine how much more of a struggle it can be for teenagers. There are some young couples and high school sweethearts that make it. They stand the test of time. Their exciting young relationship grows and develops into true love.

However, for every high school couple that remains together, there are many more that don't. And, of the couples that do get married after high school, over 50% of them get divorced before they have been married for ten years. This makes it confusing for young people. They want their relationship to last, yet they see the statistics that seem to say there's only a slight chance of that happening. This fear alone is enough to cause some to break up with each other as they prepare to transition to adulthood. The first feelings that preteens and teens usually experience are feelings of infatuation or a crush. The feelings are more intense than the young person is used to, and are easily mistaken for love. Looking back to that moment, Tapiwa could describe that moment with nothing short of infatuation between two hot blooded teenagers.

After school, the game changes. The female stays with her parents until a man asks for her hand in marriage. The Zimbabweam culture does not promote shacking up. It is shunned, and morally degrading. People usually ended up with, or married within their social class. The man is able to choose down his social class, but this rarely happens with women. She will be considered the laughing stock. Financial status is key in the dating game in Zimbabwe. The highlight in a woman's life is her wedding day. She wants the most expensive beautiful dress, a fleet of luxurious cars. An enormous cake and food people will never forget. As soon as the wedding is over, the woman is expected to become pregnant.

As the car slowed down in front of her house, Tapiwa suspended her thoughts. She paid for her fare, got out from the car and watched as the man drove off into the distance. When she was sure he was long gone, she walked up to her door. As soon as she opened the door, her nose was filled by the familiar scent of home. The insides were much warmer, and her body temperature adjusted accordingly. Taking her shoes and coat off, Tapiwa trudged to the kitchen. She grabbed a cup of water, and downed it in three gulps. She wasn't aware of how thirsty she was until she walked in. Resting against a cabinet, Tapiwa's thoughts streamed back.

Growing up, Tapiwa had a different thought to such matters. She did not dream of a fairy tale wedding, or a boisterous crowd. She envisioned a wedding on an island, with about ten people. The usual range was at least two-hundred people in Zimbabwe. Every time she started this conversation with friends and family, they would laugh at this idea, and said it could never happen in an African household. After all, humans couldn't fathom what isn't regarded as the norm. It is common to target the one who appears to be different in the most obvious ways, and direct aggression at them as an individual, or as a group. This makes them feel better, and distracts them and others from the ways in which they do not fit in. For whatever reason, humans are uninterested in differences. Internally, they are frequently filled with misplaced jealousy and discomfort.

But the culture doesn't end, before a marriage could take place in Zimbabwe, a man must pay dowry.

Chapter Five

CULTURE

Bride price, or 'roora or lobola' in the local Shona language, is the customary token paid by the groom-to-be to his future in-laws. It is seen as a token of appreciation to the bride's parents for raising a daughter. The man has to communicate with his future wife's aunt. She is the middleman during the negotiations. He has to come with representatives in form of family and friends. At least one elderly person from his family must be present. A shopping list is provided for the man to bring together with his dowry. Examples are clothes, food items and alcohol. Once the woman's family accepts the dowry, celebrations commence. The man and woman are now husband and wife. It is up to the couple to do what we refer to as the "white wedding". This is the usual first world country type of wedding. Tapiwa has seen people spend thousands of dollars in those weddings of course; Africans are known to be very extravagant.

She could remember her parents' wedding; it was the talk of the town. Tapiwa was ten when her parents finally decided to have a white wedding. When she was born, they had a simple court wedding and lobola. She liked the fact that her siblings and she could be part of the wedding. She admired the fact that they had an extravagant wedding after they had bought their home, and were financially stable. Tapiwa's mother comes from the Ndebele people; a tribe referred to as the people who bathe in milk. Because her ancestors were rich in cows, so much, that instead of bathing with water they bathed in milk. Tapiwa remembered observing from the corner as her mom was getting dressed for her big day. The great aunties came and chanted Ndebele affirmations. She could feel chills run down her spine, and could not be prouder that such a powerful culture ran through her veins.

She felt cold, but at the same time she felt the heat that raced through her veins. It was a core memory she knew she would remember as long as she lived. They partied, they ate, and they danced. It was a moment of absolute joy and pleasure. As a kid, knowing your parents was in charge of a party, made you feel a different high. Tapiwa could remember the joy she felt as people offered their congratulations. Days after the celebration, the festive atmosphere was still present, and it felt like being on a holiday. Although Tapiwa wished she had such a wedding, life had other plans for her. The first man she married was nothing like her father. Fast track to her traditional wedding, it was not close to the one she had witnessed as a kid. At about seven months pregnant, she got admitted in the hospital and stayed until she gave birth. In Zimbabwe, when such happens – if the lady has a child before the man pays dowry, he is asked to pay a damage fee. Her daughter's father ended up paying the dowry before she gave birth. He sent his family to do the negotiations, and that was it. Alone, and in pain, Tapiwa remembered looking at the pictures, but because she was not there, and was dealing with pancreatitis while pregnant – the moment did not feel exciting.

Tapiwa ached and moaned from the pain that ripped through her body. She couldn't move, she couldn't breathe. Her baby had tripled in weight, and her body bore the brunt of such change. She remembers the swollen situation of her feet, and the warm massages she had to undergo daily to lay back down. Time slowly ticked away, and the day of her due date approached steadily. Thinking back to those moments, Tapiwa knew she would go through it again, just to be her daughter's mother. Her heart swells just thinking about the bundle of joy she had help produce. Her skin, her blood, her genes, and her love – her daughter had it taken it all. The unconditional love of a mother is like nothing else in this world. It is a feeling that transcends both positive and negative, with its virtue representing human kindness, compassion, and affection.

***

Long before Tapiwa met her daughter's father, she had met many men – and had seen many things. Light skin women in Zimbabwe are at the top of the dating hierarchy. They are referred to as 'yellow bones', having one is the ultimate trophy. It is a status symbol and this is why women are pressured to bleach their skin. Tapiwa who is naturally light skinned found herself at the peak of such hierarchy. Mortifying at the lengths women went to be light skinned, the love turf was in itself a battle field.

By the time she finished high school, a new world waited for the young Tapiwa. She went clubbing and all social events. Being a yellow bone, many guys would try to get her attention; strutting around like peacocks trying to attract a mate. At a point, such attention breeds desensitization. Tapiwa got used to such notice, and as such she began to change tactics. She started to only give her attention to wealthy guys. There was one that stood out – a wealthy man that worked for the reserve bank.

The first time she heard about him was in High School. He would often throw three-day white parties. Every girl wished they could be with him. He was far from handsome, but his pockets ran deep. Tapiwa had met his employee previously at an event. He was very handsome and tall. His name was Cane. On that day, Tapiwa was waiting for her mom to pick her up at a strip mall, when she saw him again. Spotting a familiar face amidst the crowd brought a smile to her face.

"Long time no see." He greeted.

"I know right, How have you been?" Tapiwa replied. Her mind raced as she tried remembering his name, thinking back to the moment he had once told her.

"Tapiwa, right?" He said

"Yeah. And you are –" She trailed off, hoping he would fill in the blank.

"Cane." He said.

At that moment, Parai rolled down the window and said "Why would you like to be with my employee when you can be with a real boss?" Cocky it was, but his pockets backed his words. Almost like a scene from a movie, he called his bodyguard and gave him a wad of cash.

"Get her anything she wants from the food court." He orders. Following suit, Tapiwa who was wide-eyed, thanked him shyly, leaving behind an employee who knew he had lost. Tapiwa ordered a party size pizza, called a mega-licious. Feeling quite pleased, she turned around – only to catch sight of her mother.

Her heart banged loudly on her chest, a cold sweat breaking out from her temples. She knew what would happen if her mom saw her with a strange man. As her mom pulled up in the parking lot, Tapiwa quickly gave the bodyguard her number, and told him to act as if they had never met as her mom was in the parking lot. Perhaps used to such situations, the bodyguard nodded, playing along with the game of pretense. He walked away like a stranger among the crowd, not turning back as he disappeared from sight.

"Mom…" Tapiwa laughed tersely, knowing there was no place to hide such a large package.

"Did you wait long?" Her mom asked, her eyes straying to the large pizza Tapiwa was holding. Tapiwa could sense the questions before her mom said anything. "How did you get the money to buy the pizza? I know this one is expensive…" Her mom asked, quite perplexed.

"My friend and I bought it together. But she had to leave because it was taking too long." Tapiwa replied, lying through her teeth. It was the best answer she could come up with in such a short time. And as her mom looked down at the pizza she was holding once more, the nervous feeling in Tapiwa's belly doubled. It felt like her stomach was twisted into tight knots, and her mind raced for a topic she could talk about.

"Hmm, let's go then." Her mom said, turning towards the direction she had parked her car. Tapiwa followed silently, feeling weak and exhausted like she had run a thousand miles. But that was only the beginning of Tapiwa's relationship with Parai.

Parai would shower her with money; a lot to make a teenage girl go wild. Tapiwa had never seen so much hard cash in her entire life. She remembers one time he came to her parent's home with a convoy of the latest cars; all expensive brands that would cost thousands of dollars. The gifts went on and on, and slowly Tapiwa became used to collecting things from him. She once told him that her phone broke, and he said he would bring her a new one in school the next day. He brought out two grocery bags of hard cash, and said "This is your lunch money, baby girl." That was the same time Lil Wayne became popular.

The exhilarating rush of being on top of the world, money, and the giddiness that it solely belongs to her was a combination that gave her a new high. Tapiwa brought out her old phone, and started playing 'make it rain' by Lil Wayne and fat Joe.

Yeah, I'm in this b for terror got a handful of stacks
Better get an umbrella, I make it rain, I make it rain
I'm in this b for terror got a handful of stacks
Better grab an umbrella, I make it rain
I make it rain, I make it rain on them
I make it rain, I make it rain on them
I make it rain, I make it rain on them
I make it rain, I make it rain on them...

The song became Tapiwa's new anthem. A track song for how her life was going. With enough funds, Tapiwa started showering her parents employees with bank notes equivalent to their salaries. They were so happy and gave her new respect. The next day Parai came to her school and gave her a Nokia E65. There were only a few in the country at that time. From what she heard - there were only three. It was the iPhone of that time period; a high class phone of 2007. Tapiwa could hear a lunch server call out her name as she was passing the cafeteria.

"Ma?" Tapiwa said, curious about what was going on.

"Big girl!" The woman hailed. "Everyone in school is talking about your new phone. It is fire! You are really balling." The woman guffawed.

At that moment, Tapiwa could feel something sink deep in her belly. Unlike the woman's enthusiasm, she didn't feel pleased about such rumor. Instead, she felt fear, and the dread of her parents finding out about such buzz. She wondered what else people knew about her? What they thought she did to get those things? Those questions lingered in her mind. Forcing a smile, Tapiwa excused herself, hurrying off before the woman said another thing. As she walked back to her table, her skin began to prickle, and she could feel the stares boring holes into her skin. She was close to being paranoid at that moment.

Tapiwa knew that although she was getting a lot, she would probably lose things in equivalent exchange. The line was drawing near, and soon she could predict Parai would ask to sleep with her. At that time she was a virgin, and the fear of catching an incurable disease or getting pregnant made her feel terrified. Bit by Bit, Tapiwa began to ignore him. She could feel the loss, but she knew it was for the better. One of her girlfriends wanted a piece of the good life, and so Tapiwa set her up with him. Eventually, her plan worked, and she was off the hook.

Back to present, Tapiwa pushed away from the kitchen cabinet, dropping the glass cup in the sink. Sighing, she turned off the kitchen light and headed upstairs. She was tired, and she was reminded of the fact that she had to get up very early the next day. After a quick shower, a change of clothes, and a quick bite – Tapiwa turned the last light off.

It was time for bed.

Chapter Six

ANOTHER CHAPTER

Life is a journey filled with lessons, hardships, heartaches, joys, celebrations and special moments that will ultimately lead us to our destination, our purpose in life. The road will not always be smooth; in fact, throughout our travels, we will encounter many challenges. Some of these challenges will test our courage, strengths, weaknesses, and faith. Along the way, we may stumble upon obstacles that will come between the paths that we are destined to take. In order to follow the right path, we must overcome these obstacles. Sometimes these obstacles are really blessings in disguise, only we don't realize that at the time. Along our journey we will be confronted with many situations, some will be filled with joy, and some will be filled with heartache. How we react to what we are faced with determines what kind of outcome the rest of our journey through life will be like. When things don't always go our way, we have two choices in dealing with the situations. We can focus on the fact that things didn't go how we had hoped they would and let life pass us by, or two, we can make the best out of the situation and know that these are only temporary setbacks and find the lessons that are to be learned.

Time stops for no one, and if we allow ourselves to focus on the negative we might miss out on some really amazing things that life has to offer. We can't go back to the past, we can only take the lessons that we have learned and the experiences that we have gained from it and move on. It is because of the heartaches, as well as the hardships, that in the end help to make us a stronger person. The people that we meet on our journey, are people that we are destined to meet. Everybody comes into our lives for some reason or another and we don't always know their purpose until it is too late. They all play some kind of role. Some may stay for a lifetime; others may only stay for a short while.

Although Tapiwa was street smart, she was still a smart student. She passed her exams, and it was time to select universities. She was ready to open a new chapter of her life, and create new words on the new page. Her best friend was going to Australia to complete her education. Tapiwa had family in the United States, and her grandmother really wanted her to move there. Thinking things objectively, Tapiwa knew would not be focused in America, and it seemed like a lot was going on there just by watching the news. She set her heart on Canada. Her student visa was rejected the first time, but she did not give up. On the second try, Tapiwa finally got her visa. Alone, wide-eyed, full of aspirations, and scared at the same time, nineteen year-old Tapiwa left Zimbabwe to pursue a degree in finance.

***

Tapiwa had watched a lot of movies – filled with different characters and scenes. Some of the movies were about University life. Each and every one portrayed it as a place with much fun and enjoyment; a place with no boundaries, pure freedom and joy.

It was a lie.

Sure, University life gives one so much choice and independence. You chose if you go to class. You chose when, and what to eat. You chose when to sleep. But then, it takes a lot of effort. Tapiwa realized that not everything is bright and colorful. University can be extremely challenging, and on many occasions – she felt lost, not knowing where to go or what to do. It is a swamp with a lot of competition between students for top grades. University was a place where there is an extreme pressure on grades and not understanding. For Tapiwa – she had to be extremely focused. She found the nightlife boring as compared to the fast life in Harare. And worst – the song choice was mostly country music. It was a genre she wasn't used to, and over time, got sick of.

Although there were a variety of international students, the dating game had changed. The Zimbabwean men did not waste their time on Zimbabwean girls; as there were so many options to choose from. Far from a culture that shunned shagging up, Canada was a place where it was easier to hookup, or sleep with a total stranger. The yellow bone status quickly faded; and Tapiwa was just like any other girl. But then, as time passed by – Tapiwa found herself lonely on most days. She was overcome with the urge for a human connection, to feel, and to be loved. She wished she had someone like that.

In the end, she decided to have a long distance relationship with a man called Thabani. Thabani was a fling Tapiwa met after high school. And as days melded into months, and months melded into years, they ended up dating for about seven years on and off. Tapiwa had initially met Thabani at a gas station with her partner in crime Miara. They were both waiting for a cab, but then he offered them a ride. With that first meeting, relationships began to build, and soon enough, they started going to parties and clubs together. It was always him, Miara and Tapiwa – an odd trio that seemed to work out well.

On one of those days, Miara was absent – leaving Tapiwa and Thabani to their own vices. Hours of clubbing, and an hour more before Tapiwa could get home, they were both in his car – enjoying the solitude the night provided. As hormones began to run rampant, the heat and tension building with each second, they began to kiss. That was the beginning of their ill-fated romance. At that time, gas was scarce in Zimbabwe, and Tapiwa used to stay very far from the city. Thabani was the only person, no matter what, that would take the road trip and drop her off.

He was a year younger than her, street smart but not book smart. He was a spoiled, rich kid, who went to an international American school – but never took school seriously. He would take her to the most expensive restaurants, and fly her out to South Africa. To Tapiwa, a relationship with him was a thrill; a continuous and never ending moment filled with adrenaline. He was definitely the bad-guy high school girls would go for. Over the years Tapiwa matured, and realized this was not the life she wanted. She looked at his friends and family, no one was in a stable relationship. It was all fun and games, and she thought to myself 'I do not want a life full of drama.'

On Tapiwa's holiday visits to Zimbabwe, she was always confronted by women who claimed to be his girlfriend. But deep down, Tapiwa viewed the relationship as something temporary. Although they were together, and was often confronted by his infidelity – she was calmer than she should actually be. An obvious maturity to the childish countenance he showed on most days. One of the confrontations Tapiwa had with his infidelity was with a girl that was in high school.

"Leave my man alone, he doesn't want you, he is with me." The teenage girl yelled, obviously out for some chaos.

Tapiwa tilted her head to the side, viewing a child that hasn't seen a quarter of the world. She was young, she was naïve, and ultimately believed – Thabani was the one for her. Sighing, Tapiwa moved closer, a strange calmness that freaked the young girl who fought for something she shouldn't have.

"You know, you should be more focused on your education at this moment. You might regret it if you don't listen to me." Tapiwa said. Before the girl could say another word, Tapiwa left, more amused than annoyed For her, it was as easy as swatting a fly. After all, she couldn't go all out with a child.

A year passed after that, and Tapiwa was back in Zimbabwe once again. She got back to gloomy news, and the lingering taste of death. Thabani's dad was in the last stages of cancer. Tapiwa saw a different side of a man she had known for years. Although she had met his siblings, she had never met his parents. She would often go to the hospital with him, and she witnessed a distraught man trying his hardest, and spending his last penny to save his father. She watched as the darkness deep within swallowed this carefree being. Gone was his smile, in place was a darkened scowl that seemed to be engraved to his face. During this time, Tapiwa felt a myriad of emotions as she helplessly watched from his side. Tapiwa have heard and known of people that had died. But this was the first time that she was very close to the scene. She became aware of what influence death hold over another being. She could see how it tore Thabani apart, dragging him into the shadows, towards a reality he wasn't prepared to have.

Time was constantly ticking, and the days Tapiwa could spend in Zimbabwe were over. She had to go back to Canada – back to university. A few weeks after she left, Thabani's father passed away. The man had gone to rest, but the devastation he left behind was very much evident. Although she wasn't there, the cold tone of Thabani's voice spoke of a grief that ate deep into his heart. All she could do was send him money for the funeral, and ask her family to represent her. There is a saying that goes – time heals it all. Perhaps true, perhaps not true, things slowly eased back to the way it was. Tapiwa was focused on school, but the bumps of life sometimes restrained the things she could do.

Tapiwa was financially constrained. She was all alone, and the bills she had to pay kept piling up. She did her best, but sometimes the best were hard times. Thabani could not do anything for her. And it took Tapiwa a while to realize that the relationship was one way. Love without financial stability was hard. It is considered sweet and beautiful when such things happen in movies. But reality was much harsher. Every human struggled to stay afloat. She also resented the fact that throughout her four year degree, he never made an effort to visit, or come for her graduation. Tapiwa could only conclude that for a relationship to work, effort was key. To prove, the willingness, the perseverance, the tolerance to do things, to work things out... it was all thinned out when it came to Thabani and her. There was no love lost, all that was left was a chore to keep up appearances.

After she graduated, Tapiwa moved to Calgary – a city famous for hosting the largest rodeo in the world, the annual Calgary Stampede, nicknamed *"The Greatest Outdoor Show on Earth."* It is also known for its Heritage Park Historical Village, the Calgary Zoo, The Prince's Island Park, Glenbow Museum, The Bow River, The Calgary Tower, and Home to the National Music Center, Wonderland Sculpture, and the Bowness Park.

It was a fresh change, and a new beginning. There was also an oil boom going on, and Tapiwa's goal was to work for an oil company. She was able to get a three-year visa to work in Canada, after her degree.

Chapter Seven

DOWN THE HILL

The buzzing sound of an alarm clock jarred Tapiwa from her sleep. Groaning, she turned to her left, blankly staring at the wall on the opposite side. Although she was awake, her mind had yet to catch up with her body. Time slowly ticked by, until finally – Tapiwa gave in. Pushing herself up, she rested her back against the wall, sighing as she stared at the time. It was little after 6:00am, and her day was already started. She needed to get up, do some chores, and finally headed to the studio for the second day of interview.

"I swear I hate mornings sometimes." She groaned. She scrambled off the bed, leaving an imprint behind. For the next hour, Tapiwa bathed, ate and got ready just in time. Starting at her reflection on the mirror above the bathroom sink – she knew she was ready to go. She got coffee on the way, and headed straight for the studio. Unlike yesterday, Tapiwa felt much familiar with the atmosphere. She was also surrounded by familiar faces, and that diminished any form of awkwardness.

"Ms. Tapiwa." The receptionist greeted.

"Hello." Tapiwa smiled.

"You can go right up." The receptionist said, nodding her head towards the direction that led upstairs.

"Thank you." Tapiwa replied, making quick work of the steps. Without breaking a stride, she knocked Lyra's door.

"Tapiwa?" Lyra called from inside. "Hold on, one minute." She added. Tapiwa dropped the hand she was about to twist the door knob, waiting for her to be done. She could hear rustlings and hushed whispered, but couldn't make out the words that were being said. A moment later, the door opened, and a flushed Lyra poked her head out the door.

"Sorry about that." She apologized. "You can go to the studio; I will be there in a second."

"Oh, okay." Tapiwa replied, a bit perplexed. As she turned around, she heard Lyra say. "And, good morning!"

"Good morning to you too." Tapiwa responded, while walking away. The studio was the same as yesterday, except it was less noisy.

"Leto?" Tapiwa called out, but there was no reply. Walking around a bit, she had the chance to observe some of the things she had been too tense to see. Like the enormous fan that stood by the corner; how she had managed to miss it, she wasn't sure. Few minutes later, the makeup artist got started, and they were almost halfway done when Lyra came in, behind was Leto.

"Hello, Hi." Lyra greeted once more.

Tapiwa nodded, unable to talk since the makeup artist was working on her lips.

"Tapiwa, you're here." Leto greeted, running a hand through his hair. Tapiwa's response was the same, and it took only a split second as she realized something. She looked at Lyra, then back at Leto. Unable to control herself, a grin broke on her face. "Sorry." She mumbled, as the makeup artist, hovered her brush next to her lower lip. Tapiwa bit her tongue, looking away.

An hour later, they were back to the same set-up they had worked with yesterday.

"One, two, action!"

"Good morning, welcome to your number one TV station news and updates. I am your host Lyra McKinnon, taking you through this session. It is the second day of our interview with Ms. Tapiwa Sherrill, who is the co-author of the popular novel – Black Romance. Thank you for gracing us with your presence once again." Lyra said.

"Thank you for having me over." Tapiwa said, a much natural smile than yesterday.

"We will be delving deeper into the chapters. One of our popular requests is about the ending of chapter seven and the entirety of chapter eight, so we will be talking about today."

"Yeah, no problem at all." Tapiwa assured. Tapiwa grabbed a copy of the book, flapping the pages to the aforementioned chapter.

"Fantastic." Lyra responded, showing her award-winning smile.

"Chapter seven…" Tapiwa started, and once again time rewinds to the moment she had burned on those pages.

***

The nightlife became attractive once again. Calgary was different from her university's small city – Kamloops. Tapiwa would often get attention from Africans, and her confidence was at an all-time high. She was also financially stable, as she was working at an oil rig. She was making over sixty thousand a year, at just twenty-four. Tapiwa could only agree that there was no better freedom than being financially stable. She didn't have to worry much, and her life seemed to be smooth sailing. She was fully immersed into the world of the adults. She was in a state she didn't want to change.

Someone once said – if humans can predict what would happen next, perhaps we would never be sad. But at the same time, it would be pure catastrophe. Everything seemed to be going fine for Tapiwa – or so she thought. The future she couldn't predict brought along a bump she couldn't evade. The company she was working for suddenly lost its contract, and the world of the financially stable lost its balance at that moment. By the time Tapiwa heard the news, she was on holiday in Zimbabwe; living it up. Learning or hearing bad news on vacation left one with such a bittersweet feeling. Tapiwa was having fun, but occasionally, she would be reminded that the life she knew back in Canada would change once she got back. The morals Tapiwa had learned growing up, kept her calm. She had seen her grandmother pushed to the brink, and still surviving while raising six kids. For Tapiwa, her situation was nothing but a walk in the park when compared to her grandmother's. Although temporary, she left her worries at the door, and had fun while she could.

By the time holiday was over, Tapiwa went back to Canada. She began to search for another job in the same line. But it was difficult finding a job back in the oil rig. Eventually, she started working for a restoration company, and also part-time for a tax company. The clogs of her life were slowly moving on once again. She was staying in a nice high-rise professional apartment, with a roommate. But with work back in order, the problem she once faced plagued her once more – the cravings for human connection; to feel loved, to have someone to call her own. Tapiwa found herself, most times as the third wheel when her roommate went on dates.

On a Friday night, Tapiwa and her roommate were headed to a Portuguese restaurant were her roommate had a date. But coincidence, they met two Nigerian men. They were roommates.

"Hi, my name is Tao." The shorter guy introduced. "Can I get your number?" He asked, not wasting time at all. Tapiwa was never attracted to short guys. But this time, she thought 'well, it doesn't hurt to make new friends' she gave it to him for his confidence, exchanging contact information.

"What are you doing after this?" He asked.

"My roommate has a date, and I am tagging along." Tapiwa replied. At the same time, her roommate's phone started to ring. The guy she was meant to meet had stood her up.

"He is not coming." Her roommate said.

Tapiwa couldn't help but scoff as she rolled her eyes. She knew the date personally and there was one thing she knew all too well – he was cheap. Before they left the apartment, Tapiwa had placed a bet that he would not buy them lunch. And she was right.

"What did he say?" Tapiwa queried.

"He said he just made an expensive purchase, and he could not afford lunch anymore." Her roommate replied, disgust evident on her face. Tapiwa couldn't help but laugh. Tao, listening to the conversation, said "Let me make it up to you guys." And just like that, the date remained, but the man changed. They all ate at the Portuguese restaurant and by the end of the day – he dropped them off at their apartment. Surprisingly, he stayed in the same building.

As the days grew colder, Tapiwa spent more time with the Nigerian man she had met that night. But as fate would have it, another West African man found interest in her. He was tall and quite handsome, but the conversations were boring. He was someone Tapiwa would refer to as an intellect. For their date, he took her to the university library; sharing articles he found interesting. It was cute, but not something she envisioned for herself. In the end, she chose to be with Tao. After all, he was more fun, and a great cook.

But that was only at surface level. The longer you spend time with someone, the more you see things that weren't obvious at first. Tao had just graduated in Ontario. But he showed no sign or competitiveness of someone that was already in the work force. He was lazy; he would not last a month at any job. Tapiwa later realized that he was a scammer. He would travel down to the United States, and come back with a lot of money. With growing fear of being involved with things that could ruin her life, Tapiwa was already planning her escape.

Tapiwa's roommate ended up moving out, and Tao's roommate also moved out. The landlord suggested that they both become roommates, and pay rent separately. The temptation of saving money, and also skipping over the stress of finding a new roommate made Tapiwa agree. She helped Tao get a job at the restoration company she was working for; but it did not last either. It felt like they were nothing but roommates. Tapiwa did everything for herself, the only thing he did for her was cook good food. She told him it was not working anymore, and if she found someone better, she would leave. She eventually did.

It just so happened that Tapiwa's guy friend was playing match maker for his brother. Out of politeness, she decided to speak to his brother – Leo. She found the conversation boring, and he sounded very mature. Tapiwa couldn't help but picture him as an old, unattractive guy. One day, while Tao was out of town, Leo called her out of the blue. He asked what she was doing, and Tapiwa told him she was about to finish work, and head home. He asked if he could take her out for supper. She agreed and thought it was a harmless date besides her friend would see that she put effort. A Jeep rolled up by the office. A tall handsome guy came out, and gave her a hug. She told him he definitely did not look like his voice. He was also impressed as he underestimated her looks. They had a great conversation, and instantly clicked. As they were walking back to the car, he told her how good they looked together. She started seeing Leo, and eventually Tao found out. He gave her an ultimatum whether him or Leo.

Well, Leo worked in the oil rigs and he did not come to her defense. So Tapiwa chose Tao. She had blocked Leo. Valentine's Day came up, and Tao did not say anything or even buy a flower. She was so angry. She had told him she wanted to go to a Nigerian celebrity valentine's party. He just sat there on the couch. Tapiwa was disappointed. She called a Nigerian friend who lived in another building close to her. She knew he had a crush on her, so it was easy to get an invite. He invited Tapiwa to join him, and his friends for a night out. Although it was not the party she wanted to go to, she was glad she did something for Valentines.

Tao did not look for her. She bumped into Leo's brother that night, and asked him about Leo. He told her that his brother was in town. She unblocked him, and out of fun, sent him a message. He came to the club, and they ended up spending the week together until he had to go to work. It was officially over with Tao. They remained roommates and hardly saw each other. Tapiwa also hardly saw Leo, as he was chasing long days on the site. She decided to get back to her single life. Tapiwa's work permit was also expiring soon, and she was getting ready to move back to Zimbabwe. During that process, she shut down any opportunity to entertain anyone. But in the middle of such chaos, she met a man she would end up marrying, and eventually divorcing – her future ex-husband.

Chapter Eight

THE BEGINNING OF THE END, FACADES, MY FUTURE EX-HUSBAND.

Tapiwa first met Tawanda back in December 2014. He came for a party in Calgary since he lived in Edmonton. He had just finished his engineering program in Ontario. They both met on Facebook. Tapiwa noticed they had many friends in common, and it was strange to see that they had never met. During that time period, Tapiwa was emotionally unavailable. Getting off a relationship with someone that ignored, and another that was too busy left her very drained. Instead, they became good friends.

The more comfortable they became, the more she discussed about a wide range of topics – including Tapiwa's past relationships. She told him about Tao, and also the fact that she was moving back to Zimbabwe soon. For the first time, Tapiwa met someone that didn't judge, and was quite open-minded. Little by little, actions upon actions, their relationship became much closer. Tapiwa would let Tawanda crash at her place whenever he came to Calgary. He would show her his 'bachelor food', a quick staple he wolfed down when he was all alone. Tapiwa would jest about such cooking methods, and eventually end up cooking him some traditional food whenever she saw him. It was a harmless friendship, or so she thought.

But it was so easy to fall in love. It was a slow poison that penetrated ones being; unstoppable and unquenchable. They started calling each other best friends, and would talk for hours on the phone. Eventually, Tawanda started driving to Calgary every weekend. His justifications ranged from spending time with his best friend, and being jealous about potential guy best friend. At that time, Tapiwa thought it was sweet. But oh, if only she knew. If only she had set up boundaries, perhaps much heartache would have been avoided.

The time to move to Zimbabwe was drawing closer, but Tawanda was reluctant to see her go. With promises of taking care of her since he was a citizen, and the fear of losing a best friend he had grown so close to – he proposed sponsorship. Although it was a tempting offer, it was only four months into the relationship. Tapiwa declined the offer, and agreed to have a long distance relationship. Saying goodbyes were painful, as they had grown fond of each other. Tapiwa was not sure of the future, but as the popular saying goes – there is no place like home.

A month after living in Zimbabwe, Tapiwa got a job as a marketing officer and also worked for a family business. She blended in very well. An old co-worker was getting married on an island in British Columbia, Canada. She sent Tapiwa an invite, and so she applied for an American visa and a Canadian visa; she got them both. Tawanda bought a return ticket from South Africa to New York, and then she got another ticket myself from New York to Edmonton.

Together, they flew to Vancouver Island for the wedding. It was sweet and intimate. Tawanda asked Tapiwa to stay with him, and that she did not have to worry about anything. With the sweet taste of temptation and the reluctance to leave behind someone she had slowly fallen in love with – Tapiwa agreed. She stayed with him for six months, but eventually the morals instilled to her very core begin to prick her conscience. Tapiwa started to feel like a burden since she could not work. It was a suffocating feeling, surrounded by the feeling of uselessness and helplessness. Although he gave her all she needed, it just didn't feel as right as getting them with her own hands.

Feeling lost and conflicted, she had a deep conversation with him. She remembers that day as clear as night. The feeling of unease as she poured out her feelings to the man she was now in love with. She remembered how he had held her hand tenderly, pressing a kiss to the base of her palm. "Do you trust me?" He asked. "I do." Tapiwa responded, not breaking her gaze from his; she got her reply the very next day. Tawanda officially sponsored Tapiwa's stay in Canada, and a short time later- they had a small wedding ceremony.

Three months later, Tapiwa was allowed to work. She got a job at a commercial real estate company. The newly married couple was in a good place. Tapiwa remembers how many strangers would compliment them on how great they looked together. But with the sweet came the bitter. Tawanda centered his life around her. They were always together even at the gym.

Around spring time 2016, he officially proposed to her. They had a sophisticated dinner at the Fairmont Hotel, one of the most prestigious hotels in Canada. During dessert, he stood up and got down on one knee. The ring was surrounded in diamonds with one big diamond in the center. They became engaged. Technically married but engaged. Days after the engagement, Tapiwa became very sick. *What a price to pay for such delicate food.* She had ordered duck meat, and the next morning she became very nauseous. Tapiwa tried various antiemetic medications, but nothing worked. As she sat on the toilet's seat, feeling terrible and hoping the feeling went away, a sudden thought popped up in her mind. 'What if I am pregnant?' She thought.

Tapiwa laughed at the thought of being pregnant. As the days went by, she kept brushing it off. There was no way; after all, she had taken a pregnancy test and it was negative. Eventually, she went for blood tests, and the doctor confirmed the one thing she had continuously brushed off - she was indeed pregnant. It was a myriad of emotions. The feeling of excitement, fear, and the thought of bringing another human to this world was terrifying, but at the same time exhilarating.

Tapiwa lost a lot of weight during her pregnancy as she could not tolerate food. But apart from that, everything seemed to be progressing smoothly. Five months into her pregnancy, Tapiwa was lying next to her husband who was deeply asleep. She felt restless, but didn't want to wake up the man that had worked all day. With a conscious effort, she turned around and spotted her husband's phone. He had left his phone unlocked. Feeling bored, and with curiosity blossoming deep down her belly, she decided to snoop around. Tapiwa went into his Whatsapp messages, it was too clean, no sign of females, just family. She also noticed that many messages were deleted. Her sixth sense was tingling, and the detective buried within got to work. She went to another application – snap chat. It was at that moment that Tapiwa opened a can of worms.

Her heart began to race, her palms sweaty, and her throat hurting from the unshed tears that rushed to the surface. The messages revealed a secret she was never meant to see. Her husband was flirting with many women, and in graphic texts, he would describe how he would be sexual with them. With shaky hands, she checked their locations, and the reality of what might be happening caused a sharp jab by the side of her heart. She could see that some of those women were in the same city, Edmonton. Tapiwa was disgusted. *'Who is the guy lying next to me?'* She asked herself. *Is he only pretending to love me?* Different doubts began to attack her mind, but none of them could be answered.

They were recently engaged, but it was clear to see that he was not done with the streets. Biting her lower lip to stifle a whimper, Tapiwa took pictures of those messages as evidence. That night she couldn't sleep. Her throat continued to burn as she refused to cry. As the morning light crept across the sky, Tapiwa felt the rough brush of his lips against her cheeks; her husband was awake.

"When did you wake up?" He asked, his voice thick with sleep as he stretched his hands above his head. "Do you want to eat something?" He asked, lightly kissing her arm. Tapiwa said nothing, but hand him the evidence she had collected in the middle of the night. Not breaking her gaze away from his face, she watched as his expression change so fast.

"I will be sending those messages to your family, and they will know the reason why we broke up." Tapiwa said calmly. She felt nauseous as she remembered the content of those messages. They were so dirty, that she could not delete them out of her head. He would ask for their addresses, and the things he would do to them once they met.

"You got it all wrong. I was just flirting." He argued. The conversation turned sourer since her husband insisted of it being harmless fun.

But Tapiwa didn't believe it one bit. She didn't say a word to him throughout that day. That night, he had a panic attack. This was the first time Tapiwa would witness one. It looked like he was having a heart attack, as he clutched his chest, and fell on the dining floor. His breaths were rapid, and his face turned pale. It was scary moment, as desperation ran through her vein. He somewhat managed to get enough strength, as they drove to the hospital. The doctor confirmed it was a panic attack, and with an IV drip connected to his left hand. The manipulator pulled out the pity card. He begged for her to delete the messages, saying it was the only way he could become settled.

Tapiwa cried for a week straight. She could not believe this was happening. She did not have any family close by. She couldn't tell anyone. She also could not tell her friends as they would see him differently. Tapiwa did not know what to do. That kind of stress came at the wrong time. She could not eat, and then became very sick, and got admitted in the hospital. She was in and out so much at seven months, that it was decided she would have to stay in the hospital until she gave birth. During that period, Tapiwa developed pancreatitis. It was the worst pain she had ever experienced. Regret filled with anger clutched at her mind. Tapiwa told him to forget about paying her dowry. But at her vulnerable state, his words were nothing but water dousing the fire that burned within. He begged her to go ahead with it, and that it would break his parents. Being isolated in the hospital got her thinking. Her mind began to build excuses for things he had done.

'He is the only person that came to see me'

"If I stay alone with a baby, I will be all alone, and dating would be hard.'

These kinds of thoughts would randomly pop into her mind, and eventually, Tapiwa agreed for him to send his family to pay her dowry; with the Zimbabwe culture, they became traditionally married.

Their baby girl came. His mother came to visit, and then her parents. Tapiwa and her husband put up a front. To the third eye, everything was all good, and they were happy. Little did anyone know that they were sleeping in separate rooms? A year passed, and they had not been intimate. During arguments, he would turn physical, manhandling her. He was much stronger, bigger and taller. He would be gone for most of the day, and Tapiwa looked after their daughter.

One of the moments Tapiwa would never forget happened in the early hours of the morning. Earlier that night, she was excited to be going for a baby shower. In the Zimbabwean culture, only women could go for these events, so they can unwind. Tawanda was obsessive. He would follow Tapiwa to any outing she went to. She could not meet any of her girlfriends without him being present. It felt like prison.

"You might as well wear a dress too" She yelled sarcastically. She could not understand why he wanted to tag along to a women's event. When she had a baby, Tapiwa had no family to support her. She found herself depressed, and always at home because of the cruel winters. Maternity leave in Canada is a year – which meant a whole year of boredom. Tapiwa really needed a break, and Tawanda refused to watch their daughter for a few hours. Instead, he came along with her. The party went well, and just like she predicted - only women were there. The only male present was the father of the baby; who was only hanging around to make sure everything went well. Tawanda was thrilled to find him there, and gave Tapiwa a snide look, almost as if to say *'Look.'*

The formal program was in one of their rooms, turned into a dance floor. As half an hour ticked by, Tawanda told her it was time to go home.

Frustrated, and wondering if it was all a joke, Tapiwa said "I am not ready to leave. It is not like I asked for much. I just need to dance, and enjoy the music."

"You can stay if you want, but I am leaving!" He argued, and with his raised voice, he drew a number of stares their way.

"Fine, go if you want." Tapiwa said nonchalantly. "I will see him at home." She added. Joining the dance floor once again, Tapiwa pretended not to have a care in the world – but her fun was ruined. After a few songs, she decided to leave. As they were getting into the car, he blurted, "You were flirting with the DJ huh, I see how he is looking at you and you kept on dancing for him."

Perplexed and confused to how he had drawn that conclusion, Tapiwa couldn't help but laugh in a mocking manner. She remembers dancing with some women, with the DJ being at the far end corner. He said nothing after that, and the journey back home began. Midway, the argument got heated. Her husband was driving very fast on the highway. "Is he drunk?" She asked herself. Suddenly he went straight out of the highway, and Tapiwa could see her life flash in front of her for a second. They found themselves in an open land, her breathing ragged as she grabbed the seat belt tightly she could not fathom what had just happened. As she tried to gather her composure, he shouted, "See, this is you trying to kill us." He had become very impulsive, and Tapiwa knew that if there had been another vehicle or black ice they would be done for.

She looked back, and found her baby sound asleep. It made her so sad to see her husband behave this with his daughter at the back. She was glad her daughter was still young to understand what was going on. Tapiwa's heart was beating so fast. She could feel the adrenaline rush. "Calm down, be strategic," She repeated to herself, over and over. She slowly became numb for the rest of the way home. He kept on talking about the DJ. Noticing how quiet she had become, he yanked the seatbelt, grabbing her hard on the shoulder. "I am calling the police" she shouted, her eyes blurry from the tears that were waiting to spill over. He laughed because he knew she wouldn't. He continued to harass her until they pulled into the drive way.

As soon as he pulled the car into the driveway of their townhome, Tapiwa quickly opened the car door. She fell to the ground and wept for the life she lived. She wept for her soul, which was filled with regret. If this was marriage, she did not want any parts of it. She sunk her bare hands into the earth and cried. "I do not have a husband anymore." He banged the door of the car, and found her on the ground. As he stared at her, he watched on like he had seen a ghost. Deep down, he probably knew that the universe had heard her cry. She was tired. She could not recognize him anymore. He was not the man she had met back in 2014. At that moment, Tapiwa emotionally left her ex-husband, Tawandai. Her body followed soon after.

Months later, they hit rock bottom. Tapiwa knew if she stayed any longer, one of them would not come out alive. Staring out through the window, Tapiwa decided they needed a break. Tawanda had this idea that traveling was a waste of money. Tapiwa was already depressed, and knew he would not give in to her demands. She decided to buy him and their daughter an all-inclusive trip to the Dominican Republic.

Once they got to the resort, Tapiwa was carrying their daughter, and somehow dropped the room key on the way to their room. There was a bell man helping them with their luggage. When they got to the door, Tapiwa could not find the key. Tawanda began to swear at her, and told her how stupid she was in front of the Bell man. This time, Tapiwa was not taking his insults; especially since they were out of his comfort zone. She told him he should have stayed back in Canada. The least he can do is be nice since he did not pay for the trip. The argument got so bad, the bell man left and came back later on. Tapiwa felt like she was in one of those reality shows. Why was she so triggered by him? He surely knew how to press the buttons to get a reaction out of her. She did not see herself traveling with him anymore; they just could not get along. Tapiwa knew she had to get out. Their relationship was at an all-time low.

By the time they got back home, Tapiwa was greeted with devastating news. Miara, her partner in crime when she was in high school, had passed away. They used to be inseparable. Tapiwa heard she was killed by her partner. Her heart went out to her daughter. She did not want to end up down that road. Tawanda lacked emotional intelligence. He made the death of her friend about him. Instead of comforting her during her grief, he found any reason to start an argument. When a relative of his passed away, Tapiwa returned the karma he had dished out. She treated him the same as he had done during her time of grief. Although Tapiwa gained temporary pleasure for doing such, her heart ached at the thought of what they had become. They could not be there for each through the lows anymore. At this point, there was nothing left to hold her back

Tapiwa's strategy was to convince Tawanda to let their daughter leave the country, to her parents. She became really nice to him, cooked him good meals, and created an illusion of a fairy tale. With such tactics, she convinced him to let their daughter be with her parents, so she could work harder, and they could buy a house. Tawanda liked the idea because he knew Tapiwa was good with money. During that period, she found ways to increase their income and credit scores. Before her maternity leave was over, they sat with a lawyer and did the necessary paperwork.

With her plans in play, Tapiwa took their daughter home. Although it was hard leaving her, she knew it was for the best. Tapiwa casually dropped hints about the idea of a separation to her family to test the waters on their reaction. There is a common saying in Shona that goes - 'Ndogarira vana'. It is a phrase often said by married women. It means 'when all else fails, you stay for the children.' Every response her family made was centered on her daughter. Sentences such as – 'If you leave her father, maybe your daughter would be mistreated by his new wife.'

Divorce is not widely accepted in the Zimbabwe culture. It is often the last resort. Families will do their best to keep a couple together, but in Tapiwa's case; she did not have that disadvantage. Being in Zimbabwe for Christmas 2018 was healing. She had time to reflect. There was so much love, and family; she missed that. She thought 'maybe all I needed was a break from my husband'. She also heard different stories about couples who had actually faced plenty of infidelity, and harmful physical abuse. Tapiwa started to think – 'maybe I was overreacting?' She began to second guess her choices, and once again – her mind was prepared to come up with excuses.

Tawanda was regarded as an angel to people outside their home. People always thought he was so kind. Tapiwa's reason for considering leaving was not tangible to such people. Men cheat all the time, most women said. Tapiwa believed that the universe had another lover for her, not a person but a new passion. She was suddenly motivated to start a business, and go back to school to pursue a different career. Before she left Zimbabwe, she met a lady who was selling home products. She was humble. Tapiwa noticed how high quality the products were. Tapiwa asked if she didn't mind sharing where her products came from. She told Tapiwa that they were from the United Kingdom. They began to converse, and Tapiwa learned that the woman owned many properties. Tapiwa was intrigued; she wanted her kind of life.

The woman explained how she spent six months in the UK; working as a nurse, and then another six months running her business. Tapiwa could picture herself in the woman's shoes. It was a perfect balance. Tapiwa couldn't help but tell her how much she admired her. She was also a single mother.

"I always wanted to run from the Canadian winter, and just be around for the summer." The woman said, "If you can learn anything from me, I advise you to go for nursing. This career allows you to be flexible. You can work as much as you want, and take time off as much as you want. There is always work." The woman advised.

Taking her advice seriously, Tapiwa met up with a cousin that lived in the UK. He had been in Zimbabwe for four months, and he was also running a business back home. And then, she realized that first world countries were a great place to raise capital, and business was the way to go back home. It also helped that regulations were low in Zimbabwe. Tapiwa fell in love with the idea. The universe started putting people in her path, who she aspired to be. She left Zimbabwe in January, with a new motivation, and the eagerness to become a business owner no matter how small the business was.

Chapter Ten

TRAINING GROUND

Sighing, Tapiwa closed the book. Almost immediately, the room burst into an encore, clapping vigorously as they all stared at her. Tapiwa was shocked, and at the same time – a bit embarrassed. "Thank you." She said shyly, staring at the ground.

"Wow... that's very educative in so many ways." Lyra said.

Tapiwa nodded. Few minutes after that, they wrapped up the interview, and She was facing the cold wind once more. The sun was going down, tainting the sky with an orange hue. As Tapiwa stared at the sky, she couldn't help but think that the sun had set the world on fire. It was a beautiful moment to breathe in. "The next chapter is my favorite though." Tapiwa muttered.

Time moved into the past once more, and Tapiwa imagined herself on the beaches of Tulum, Mexico. "What do you look for in a man?" Nate asked as they walked away from the breathtaking beach shores in Tulum. Tapiwa paused for a moment, thinking about it. Despite all the men she had been with, the first thing that popped up in her head was the image of the man next to her. He was six feet tall, humble and God fearing. "Tall, humble and God fearing." She replied, spilling her thoughts. Tapiwa's list used to have fifty qualities. Although it was quite unrealistic to find a man with everything; subconsciously, she had followed through with some of the things on her past list.

Although she had not known Nate for a long time, he already had these qualities and even more. Tapiwa's heart began to race the more she thought about it. She wondered if she was still in a dream. She wondered if it was possible to find such person; it still felt unreal. If Tapiwa had to describe the man she wanted to be with, it would be Nate to the tee. He was so knowledgeable, older than she was, wanted more children, and was spiritual. She also loved his taste in music. To top it off, they once worked in restoration, had a passion for travel and real estate. The more her thoughts went haywire, Tapiwa's mind would immediately delete the thought. '*How would that work if they were from two different worlds?*' '*Even if they wanted to be together, could a long distance relationship work?*' Many thoughts raced in her head, and subconsciously she had grown quiet.

"Tapiwa?" A voice called gently next to her. It was Nate. "What's wrong?" He asked.

Tapiwa smiled, shaking her head. "Nothing." She replied. Although she had so many doubts, and thoughts, she knew she had it keep it down. All she could think of was the moment they currently shared. The important thing was in that moment, all Tapiwa had to think was that, she had met the type of man she wanted to be with, and when they eventually parted ways, she would find comfort with the fact that he existed somewhere out there. "Let's go." Tapiwa said, holding on to Nate's hand. Her main reason for being in Mexico was to rest. Tapiwa had adopted the power of having no expectations. All she wanted was sun and the beach. The rest was going to be a bonus. She also wanted to sleep as much as she could, since she had spent sleepless nights in nursing school.

Tapiwa remembered the call that had followed after Krystal had called that night. It was her friend Erma. She had called right after, and as they discussed a number of things, she had finished her sentence with "I like the new you, you are taking care of yourself, and traveling." That one statement caught her attention, leaving Tapiwa shocked, but at the same time – pleased to hear that she was slowly evolving.

"Tapi, do you know you have ripened?" Erma asked. \

Tapiwa was confused. "I have ripened?" She repeated. "What does that mean."

"This might sound cringe, but Tapiwa… you have healed. You have become softer and more feminine. What is left is for your soul mate out there to find you. I just know this is your time." Erma explained. Tapiwa fell silent, warmth washing through her veins. As she let out the air she was holding in her lungs, she nodded. Although her friend couldn't see her movement, Tapiwa felt she just had to do it. "Thank you." She whispered. A second later, the line fell silent.

Her friend was right. Tapiwa could feel it. She could feel the change that was taking place. She could see that the Tapiwa she once knew – stuck in a marriage that breed contempt, depression and distraught was no more. She had truly healed. "But then, why do I keep meeting Mr. Wrong?" She muttered, running a hand across her face. When she was with Tawanda, she either blocked or stopped talking to men who showed any interest in her. And now they were no longer together, she kept herself busy. If Tapiwa was being truthful to herself, she was emotionally unavailable. She had needed that time to heal. She was in a phase where she was not entertaining even the slightest red flag that shows up in the beginning.

Tapiwa began to travel more, and would often work overtime, but still trouble found her. She became curious about the men she was once with, or would potentially date in the past five years – but they were either married or had families. Throughout Tapiwa's marriage, Leo kept in touch with her. Knowing he was married as well, they kept conversations general. Although he would end conversations saying 'he misses her' and loves her'. Tapiwa never reciprocated. She knew the effects cheating had on your married spouse. She had been there, and she knew she would never create such pain on another woman. But sometimes, Tapiwa would day dream about what ifs. *'What if we had worked out?'* She would think.

Leo would sense the slightest mood changes, it was as if he was always on the sidelines, waiting for an opportunity. Eventually, he broke things off with his partner, and the constraints that held them down were slowly diminishing. They talked more often. Sooner or later, Tapiwa was going to have to see him.

The day finally came. Tapiwa was in Halifax to see a few friends, and she had no choice but to tell Leo she was in town. Her cousin had dropped her off by her Airbnb, and in a split moment – Leo parked behind him. It was an odd coincidence, and it almost felt like his car had been trailing behind. As she hugged her cousin goodbye, she took her bags, and walked to where Leo stood. As she drew closer to him, he hugged her, and lifted her in the air. It was just like before. The chemistry remained the same – a low sizzling burn that was quite apparent. He looked the same; aging was kind to him. They decided to drive two hours back to his city. Since they were both old souls, they enjoyed old acoustical music on their way. For years, the thought would linger in her mind. *'What if I married Leo?'*

Leo was the complete opposite of Tawanda. He did not act the way Tawanda did, where everything was tied to having a better future. There was a clear difference between someone raised on love, and someone raised on survival. Leo was raised on survival. It was sad not being able to live the moment with him, but bicker on money they spent on an outing. After that trip, Tapiwa flew to see him again. And eventually got the confirmation she needed. She confirmed that he was not the one. They only enjoyed spending time together, but it was not enough to build a future on. They had many differences. Leo would not open up to her about his past marriage, or his career, or finances. What they had felt like a spiritual tie.

Suddenly, her feelings for him went out of the window. He was not the person she wanted to be with. It was one thing to look good together, but another to be happy. Tapiwa had lived through that, and she wasn't about to make the same mistakes. Everything they had was in the moment, but she knew eventually – those moments would run out. They kept in touch for a few months, and eventually stopped talking. Relationships were such weird things. One moment, total strangers became the closest to you, and the next minute – you are back to being total strangers. Tapiwa was glad she had gotten Leo out of her system for good. It was fun while it lasted, and it definitely added to the dynamics she called love.

Back to present, Tapiwa checked the time on her phone, temporarily distracted as an uber slowed down in front of where she stood. Tapiwa watched as the driver rolled down the window, poking his head out. "Ms. Tapiwa?" He called out.

"What are the odds?" She muttered beneath her breath. The driver was the same as the last time. Tapiwa stared at him for a few seconds, wondering if he remembered her. But then again, his blank expression showed nothing. Tapiwa wasn't surprised. She could only imagine the amount of passengers he dealt with in a day. "Yes. That's me." She responded, taking a picture of the car, the license plate and the driver. As she glanced back up, she caught the quick change in the driver's face. Tapiwa once again wondered if he remembered her now.

Although she had not deleted the previous pictures from her gallery, once again – there was nothing like being too careful. As soon as the car began to move, she leaned backward, resting her head against the head rest. Rolling the window down, the wind slapped against her face, causing her nose and cheeks to sting. Different thoughts began to float through her mind, and slowly her mind focused on one. The biggest feeling was Vertigo. She felt like she was repeating the scenes all over again. It felt like she was reliving moments she had once experienced. "Did I do the same thing yesterday?" She couldn't tell.

It wasn't the first time she had relived the past. But there was one time she had been actively connected to the time period. Two years ago, she found herself scrolling through old pictures from 2014. Tapiwa stumbled across a picture of the West African who pursued her before she met John- the nerd that had shared articles for a date. It was a picture captured at his friend's house for a barbeque. In the picture,

70

Tapiwa was holding a bottle of Smirnoff, and the man next to her was gazing into her eyes.

'Wow we look happy'. She thought. She asked herself how she let him go. He was well built, tall and handsome. He was an intellect. Back then, she had chosen Tao over him because he seemed too boring. At that time, he was doing a Master's Degree, and Tapiwa was fresh out of university. With the stress of exams, the freedom of never going to a class, the last thing Tapiwa wanted to see back then was another article. He loved to give her articles and ask for feedback. As the papers began to pile up, Tapiwa would give them to her Kenyan roommate to read, and also to help summarize.

Looking back, Tapiwa could finally agree that he had his own charm. She was ready for a man like him, but it was too late. Those memories were over five years ago. 'Oh well' She sighed, flipping the picture album. She realized she had a lot of his pictures. The next one was a picture of him when he was in Europe. Back then, he had promised a trip to Italy and France. He had once lived in England, before he relocated to Canada. Tapiwa could not stop thinking about that picture, and how good he looked. She went through an old phone, and found his contact. She was curious about how he currently looked, and she was certain he was married by now.

As the seconds ticked louder, her curiosity bloomed like the late flower in June. The 'what ifs' began to appear, and in the end – Tapiwa gave in to her curiosity. She eventually devised a plan to innocently get to talk to him.

As she stared at his number on the screen, she felt nervous and at the same time excited to know what her probing would lead to.

Gathering enough courage, she sent the first message. "Hi Joanne, I will be in Calgary soon. I was wondering if I could schedule a hair appointment." She typed.

Subconsciously, Tapiwa began to bite the nails of her left hand. She wondered if he would reply. She wondered if he would ignore it. But to her surprise he responded.

"I am sorry, my name is John. But if you are looking for a hair supplier, I know two females that can do your hair." He texted. Tapiwa felt her heart race as she read the words over and over. He was still polite, and that made her grin.

"Thank you." She replied, "My name is Tapiwa." She added. Unfortunately, John did not recognize her. His replies were brusque, and he treated her like she was a stranger. Tapiwa could only guess he saved her contact, since she could now see his profile picture. But that was the end of the thrilling moment, or so she thought. A month later, he messaged her. His disbelieve at not realizing who she was all along were quite evident in the text he sent. John could not believe he had found her.

"I wondered for years where you went." He sent. Few minutes later, he called Tapiwa, and they spoke for hours, catching up on what had happened in the last few years. Tapiwa learnt he had a really good job, and seemed to be doing exceptionally well. Months passed, and they kept in touch here and then. One day, John informed Tapiwa that he was going to see some friends close to her city. He said it was a party, and wondered if she wanted to tag along. Tapiwa agreed. She missed West African food, and it had been a while since she painted the town red.

Since Tapiwa was meeting John for the first time in five years, she took extra care of her appearance. It was something that was just there – the idea of looking of her best while meeting an old acquaintance. Later that night, John pulled up in the driveway, in a Porsche SUV. Tapiwa could see the perplexed expression of her roommate. They both watched discreetly from the window as he came to the door. Breathing in deeply, Tapiwa went downstairs, opening the door before he had the chance to knock. Happiness, joy, excitement and reunion rolled through the air. John gave her a hug, and afterwards grabbed her weekend bag.

Tapiwa followed behind him, trying to hide her shock. He was much more muscular, and smelled good. She couldn't help but tell him how proud of him she was. During the drive, they listened to afro beats and headed to his friend's house. John asked her where they could party. Tapiwa in time, called a guy friend who coincidentally had a birthday party. They headed over there. They enjoyed the party, and Tapiwa couldn't help but dance the night away. He was calm, sitting on the couch while taking videos of her. So often, he would chat with the people that came his way, networking. Tapiwa didn't mind being his friend, and knew she would love to do this from time to time. It was fun, until Tapiwa's ex-husband got the word that she was at the party. The mention of his name did nothing but sour the mood and ambience they had built up over the night. In the end, she decided to leave with John. On the drive back, Tapiwa told him about all the drama with her ex.

With the smooth engine, the close confines, and a friend Tapiwa felt comfortable with - they had a heart to heart conversation. John told her it did not work out with his ex-wife as well, and so he had taken time off to heal and focus on his career. As the ride finally ended, they arrived at his friend's house, and for the next few hours - they played some music and danced. While taking a break, they sat on the couch and cuddled. They talked about the 'what ifs'. How it could have been if she had chosen him instead of Tao. In the end, they kissed for such a long time. She kept thinking about the picture. They had never been intimate before, and when it happened Tapiwa found herself liking him. The next day, they spent the day indoors, watching movies and ordering food. He was now thirty-nine, and they both could not party like before. Being with him boosted her confidence. He was the perfect man. They tried to see each other at least every three months, but Tapiwa was really busy with nursing school.

She went to visit him for thanksgiving, and was amazed by his house. It was a modern, brand new house, with top notch furniture. She couldn't help but wonder why he was single. He seemed to have it altogether. What was missing was affection. He wasn't the same sweet John she met a few years back. His past relationship really must have changed him, or maybe Tapiwa never knew him that well. The atmosphere seemed so tense; she could not point her finger at the problem. Her last visit was Christmas time. They got each other gifts, they both cooked, and his son came for Christmas. Everything was so formal. Tapiwa didn't want that for herself. She wanted to be free with her partner. She wanted to show affection. With John it felt like a movie script, and it did not feel authentic. Tapiwa could not be herself, and her etiquette was at its best.

By the time she went back home, she kept giving him excuses of why she could not see him, and eventually communication stopped. John built a life for himself by himself. Tapiwa realized she lost the opportunity years ago, and because she was not going to bring anything to the table, all she was going to be was a trophy wife to him. The John she knew was no longer there, and she could not help but feel sad about it. But eventually, she got the closure she needed. In the end, Tapiwa had no one from her past she wanted to rekindle with. She was certain she would refocus on her school, and business. But fate was bringing a different stranger her way. Tapiwa decided to respond to some of her Face book messages. She began to chat a lot more with one of her friends named Isaac. In the end, she decided to scan his profile. Tapiwa realized he lived in Canada, Montreal. Months later, she had a week break from school, and it was a public holiday. She jokingly looked at the tickets, knowing they were unreasonable as it was a holiday. They were going for $1000 and up. Isaac asked if he could book her a ticket, so she would come over. Tempted by the lure of a festive day, Tapiwa sent him her information. Minutes later, he sent her a ticket. She was surprised.

Talking to her girl friends about the situation, the conclusion was either he was really serious, or he has a lot of money to splurge.

Chapter Nine

LESSONS

"Should we take a break?" Lyra asked, breaking through the fog that surrounded Tapiwa's mind. The whole studio had remained silent as she read from the chapter. Tapiwa looked down at the page she was, looked back up, and then nodded. "A break won't hurt." She replied. Almost immediately, the once quiet atmosphere turned chaotic, and Tapiwa watched with an amused expression as some of the staff scrambled out of the studio. 'I guess they really needed that break,' she thought. As soon as the microphone attached to her blouse was removed, Tapiwa stood to stretch her legs. The feeling of content as her joints were ironed out made her grin as she continued to stretch.

Dropping her hands to her side, Tapiwa's stomach let out a sound that signified hunger. Although she had eaten before she left home, she couldn't help but feel a bit hungry. In the end, Tapiwa decided to leave the studio to find something to eat.

"Do you need something?" Lyra called out.

"Uhm, I thought I might get something to eat before we resumed the interview."

"Oh, you don't need to go far, you can ask Charles to get you anything you." Myra replied, signaling for someone behind Tapiwa.

"I can just go by my–

"No, no, it is no bother. Just let –" Lyra paused, holding the left arm of the woman that just appeared. "Hayley would get you whatever you want." She completed. Feeling a bit uncomfortable, Tapiwa finally agreed. Hayley turned out to be a big fan of her work; and the young lady was all too delighted to help out where she could.

Thirty minutes, fully fed, and bursting new found energy, Tapiwa was ready for the rest of the interview. Within ten minutes, the entire staff was back on set.

"One, two, action."

Time was once again reversed to the past

***

Tapiwa had just turned thirty when she arrived back in Canada. She was kid free, and had plans for her birthday trip to Las Vegas. She was fueled with a different kind of motivation, and her trip to Las Vegas was the first step to opening a new chapter. Tapiwa remembered opening the door to the townhome she lived with her husband. It didn't feel like home; but an unfamiliar place that was colder than Antarctica.

"You are back." Her husband greeted.

"Hmm…" Tapiwa responded,

"How are people back home?" Tawanda called out to her.

"Good." Tapiwa responded, closing the door of the bedroom she slept in, sitting at the edge of the bed, she sighed. The moment was suffocating. The moment she walked past those doors, she could feel an invisible pressure weighing down on her. With a thud, she fell backwards, staring at the familiar ceiling above. "I miss my daughter." She mumbled.

Getting back up, Tapiwa poked her head out of the door, and said. "I am going to Las Vegas for my birthday trip."

"You are?" Tawanda replied, obviously in the next room. Tapiwa could hear sound of hurried footsteps, followed by the appearance of her husband by the doorway.

"You are going to Las Vegas?" He repeated.

"Yeah." Tapiwa replied.

"When are we going?" He asked.

"We?" Tapiwa repeated, frown knitting between her brows. "I am going alone." She said.

"Alone? Why?

"Tawanda, please I just got back from a long trip; I truly do not want to argue. Besides, you haven't forgotten our trip to Dominican Republic? It was a disaster; we will end up arguing most of the trip."

"You see, you already thinking negative even before we tried. You are always doing that. And then –

"I am tired." Tapiwa cut in, staring straight at his eyes. "I am tired." She repeated, closing the door of her bedroom.

For the next few days, Tawanda tried the only tactics he could use. He took Tapiwa on a shopping spree, but Tapiwa wasn't fooled in any way. Before leaving Zimbabwe, she had promised not to give in to doubts. She had also promised not to let her emotions control her thoughts. She already saw a darker side of the man she once loved. There was no going back.

In the end, Tapiwa went to Las Vegas alone. It was a fun trip, with evidence of what money could buy. When she got back to Edmonton, Tawanda and Tapiwa were slowly getting back to a good place. They started being intimate again. It made Tapiwa think, 'maybe he was not ready for a child.' It was back to how it was when they first met. Valentine's Day came. He booked a nice hotel suite, and decorated it with roses and chocolates. And despite all odds and pep talks she had once told herself - Tapiwa was slowly forgiving him.

Their church had a Valentines couple's night they attended. Their relationship was never the same after that night. The night seemed to be going well. Tapiwa was on her phone, taking videos and selfies. In the blink of an eye, Tawanda stood up in front of church members, grabbed her phone, and went on a rant about she didn't make him feel special.

'The monster in him couldn't keep away for long' she thought to herself. She was now nonchalant about his actions; she was now used to this, and she had enough. The next day, she told him she was leaving him. He could see she had grown resilient. She had nothing to lose if she left him. Everything he had was in her name, from the furniture, and the car he drove. The house, even the clothes he wore were all bought by Tapiwa. The only thing he leverage on, was calling immigration, and telling them she had done a fraud marriage.

Tapiwa wasn't fazed. She stared right back at him, not breaking a stride as she told him to go ahead, and when the lease was over she was leaving. The manipulator was at work once again. He would take pills and tell her he would kill himself. Tapiwa had no choice but to reach out to his family about this. They went for counseling in the church, but it seemed the more effort they put into fixing their relationship, the worse it got. It was a lot to take on. Over time, Tapiwa started working in mental health, and saw and learnt about various personalities. Tawanda definitely suffered from a mental disorder. She was aware of how he acted once he didn't get his way; and how he would make her pay for it. Everything was always her fault.

Most times, Tapiwa would watch as her husband put on a pity party. He would be on the kitchen floor crying; a way to gaslight her into thinking she was at fault. She simply had no capacity to carry on.

There was only one thing to keep her mind off the problems she had – to keep busy. Tapiwa started a business in beauty products, and also the initial proceedings for nursing school. She kept herself very busy. She had no time for Tawanda's antics. They lived like roommates. He offered to pay her to stay with him, but that solution was rock bottom. It was like a marriage of convenience or a friend with benefits situation. It was not working. The sex felt like a chore. Tapiwa pictured herself as a woman starring in an African movie; an actress who had to be intimate with an old man for money, while having zero emotion or orgasm. She was only thirty years old, surely she could do better. Having a child together did not motivate her to stay. She could not imagine having another child with him. Once the lease finished, she decided to go through the seperation, and move to a new town.

***

Tapiwa moved with a bag of clothes, and nothing more. It was like starting life from scratch again. She moved into a basement; since it was the only thing she could afford at the moment. Although she missed the nice house, she had a nice car; and most importantly - her freedom. It was priceless. She kept herself busy. Loneliness started to creep in. She had thoughts, and doubts about the decision she had made. 'Did I make a wrong decision?' She sometimes thought. But his behavior determined otherwise. She had tried her best, but Tawanda just wasn't it. Whenever he saw women who were light skinned, or someone with the same structure as Tapiwa, he would send the pictures to her, and say 'I am coming to your work place.' It was nothing but childish antics that irritated her to no end. On other days, he made threats using the immigration matter. His actions killed the doubt she had every time. Tapiwa was sure she had made the right decision.

The childish threats continued for a long time, and some other days it delved into stalking. Tapiwa remembers the first time he had sent a picture of her at a party to her family. To her, his actions were nothing short of immature tantrums. Three years later, Tapiwa decided the marriage was irreconcilable, and it was time to start the divorce proceedings. The only thing that held her back for three years was the expensive procedure. She was also a student, and the fear of not being able to afford it – hovered on her mind. Through grit, and perseverance, Tapiwa got the funds she needed. As she sat in the lawyer's office, signing the document that would legally grant her the freedom she wanted, she felt the weight off her shoulders, and finally she could smile.

Tapiwa knew she could not describe herself as the perfect wife. She had her faults. But then again, life was a big amusement park. Her marriage with Tawanda taught her a lot. The married life was simply not a walk in the park. Their foundation was not strong. They never discussed finances, raising children, and love languages. He was far from her type in what she looked in a man. Tapiwa knew she did not respect him. He never gave a chance to, and his deeds created more cracks, and produced more flaws.

Academically, she was smarter than him. Tapiwa had often felt that she could not learn anything from him. It didn't help that his English was not that good. At the beginning of their relationship, when she was blinded by love, Tapiwa loved to read. But her ex-husband preferred to read social media scandals. Tawanda liked to have a bad boy image, and used to boast about his street credit back in Toronto. Tapiwa was much mature as she had experienced the fast life at an early age. A want for a bad boy fades as women mature.

There were seven lessons she took from the marriage she had with Tawanda:

1. Forgive! She had a hard time forgiving. Tapiwa could not let things go and would often bring up the past in arguments. This was her biggest weakness. She realized there was no perfect man. Humans naturally make errors, including herself. Had she humbled herself to be the bigger person, perhaps it could have worked out.

2. Financial transparency. In her parents' generation, the husband would bring his salary to his wife, and the wife would distribute the money. Tawanda and Tapiwa kept their money separately. He paid the rent, and she managed the bills. The only thing they paid together was food. When they had their baby, he could not afford formula or diapers. Tapiwa was the one who had to lend him money. She got tired one day, and said no. He started asking his friends for money. She thought all was well until one day she went to deposit money into a savings account which was an emergency fund for her siblings. Tapiwa was in shock to find out there was no money in there. She asked for a year's transaction sheet to track what happened. Unfortunately, she had forgotten it was a joint account. Tawanda had taken all the money. When she confronted him, he said he was short of money. Tapiwa was very angry, and this made the trust worse.

When she worked in real estate as an administrator, Tapiwa was making $2000. Three quarters of her paycheck went to maintaining their lifestyle. They lived a life they could not afford. They had an expensive townhome with absurd bills. They had a fancy car, and Tawanda was paying off two car loans. Barely able to hold on, they also had to build a life for their daughter. It was an additional $1000 on daycare a month. A lot of issues came from financial stress. But as always, he liked to keep up appearances. Tapiwa once suggested cutting costs of expensive rent and bills by living in a one bedroom, and then they would have a large down payment for a house. Tawanda said it would not work for him, and it eventually became something she ended up doing on her own. A year after their separation, he told her he was getting evicted, and asked for money. Tapiwa told him she did not have it, and the insults continued.

3. Respect. She found it difficult to give Tawanda the respect he deserved as the head of the house. Tapiwa was an argumentative person in nature. She loved to debate in school, and she found herself winning during their arguments; a thrill that felt like a price. She made sure she always had the last say. But in relationships, Tapiwa realized that such competitiveness was unnecessary. The important thing was listening to understand. She listened to win. Tawanda did not have much confidence, so when they met other people during discussions – he would keep quiet. Respect is a good foundation to a solid marriage.

4. Quality time. Tawanda and Tapiwa during the dating phase would go out for dinners, movies. This stopped when they had their daughter. They were busy with their separate lives, and did not spend time together. This led to a marriage that felt like they were roommates. Tapiwa would make sure she worked nights, or evenings or weekends so they did not have to cross paths. Traveling is one of her love languages. They hardly traveled together. She found herself taking many trips on her own after she had left their daughter back in Zimbabwe. Tapiwa wondered if this could have been a way they could have reconnected. Traveling was more of a glimpse at how it would be if she left him. Tapiwa felt happier, and this was one of the reasons she eventually left.

5. Reassurance. Tapiwa remembered arguing so much she eventually did not remember a time she reassured him. After she discovered the flirting, during the time she was pregnant; that perhaps, must have been the last time she told him she loved him. She no longer spoke life into the marriage. The tongue is a powerful tool. They hardly complimented each other. Without reassurance, there is no

hope to carry on. It is hard to get back to where it all began, and how they wanted their future to be.

6. Goals. Although they were married, they very much lived separate lives. They never sat down and planned their lives, or set goals. Tapiwa was a meticulous planner. She would keep a diary, and have daily, weekly, monthly and yearly goals. Looking back, Tapiwa realized she did not include him into her goals. They weren't working towards the same goal. There was a lack of structure. Their plans were always in passing; an impromptu decision they had to get over with. They never planned the steps to achieve any goals.

7. Space. Tapiwa had difficulties setting boundaries with Tawanda. Vice versa, he lacked having his personal time. They were always together. It drove her crazy. He did not understand that she had basically stayed alone in Canada for seven years, and she was used to being alone. Tapiwa was not a clingy person. She hardly cuddled in any of her previous relationships. She was not used to physical touch. And with Tawanda, they never really learnt each other's love languages. Tapiwa was selfish, and also did not try to learn his love languages. Tapiwa realized that it is important to set boundaries in the beginning, because old habits die hard.

Although Tapiwa remembered more of the bad than the good, she was grateful for all the lessons. Every little thing she went through added to her character development. Everything she went through made her what she was today. She always tried to remember the good in people. There were some good times and qualities Tawanda had. But like they say, some people come into our lives as lessons or to stay. For Tapiwa, Tawanda was a lesson.

Chapter Eleven

RUDE AWAKENING

Tapiwa retraced her step on the path she had walked for two days. Today was the final interview. Although she had only been with the staff for a short period, Tapiwa felt a bit sad to finally leave. Every moment they had shared felt longer than the three days she had spent. It seemed everyone also felt that way, since the mood was a bit drab.

"Ahhh, it is the last one. We sure will be sad to see you go." Lyra said, echoing the thoughts on everyone's mind.

"Yeah." Tapiwa replied, her lips curved into a wistful smile. The makeup artist took a much longer time, and by the time she was done – Tapiwa could see that she had put in extra efforts. "Wow." She muttered, staring at her reflection in the large mirror next to her. Since she had slept late last night, Tapiwa had woken up with bags under her eyes. But now, they were non-existent. She wasn't the same person that had walked through the doors a few hours ago. "Thank you." She said, turning to look at the makeup artist. "Thank you Sandra." She said, finally mentioning her name.

Hovering at the corner was an anxious Hailey. She was holding on to a copy of the black romance, and it was not hard to deduce what she wanted to ask. "Is something wrong?" Tapiwa asked.

"Uhm, Ms. Tapiwa, can I get an autograph?" She asked.

"Oh," Tapiwa replied, warmed running through her chest. She knew what Hailey wanted, but it was still nice to hear it out loud. "Do you have a pen?" Tapiwa asked.

"Oh yeah." The younger lady rushed, moving forward. "I brought a pen." She said, stretching it out for Tapiwa to take.

Tapiwa had never really practiced an autograph to use in situations like this. Heck, she never knew the book would get this popular. Nate was receiving as much attention as she was getting, but she wondered if it was much calmer back in America. "Here, done." She said, returning the book back to her.

"Thank you so much." Hailey replied, clutching the book to her chest like it was some family heirloom.

"It's almost time." Lyra said, popping her head through the door. "Are you guys done?"

"Yeah." Tapiwa and Sandra chorused. Tapiwa's gaze caught Sandra's, and almost immediately she couldn't help but look away. She bit down on her lower lip, trying hard not to laugh. But all was for naught; Sandra was the first to give in, her throaty laughter filling the air. Letting go of the control she held, Tapiwa couldn't help but laugh alongside.

Few minutes later, the show was ready to roll. "One, two, action!"

"Good morning, welcome to your number one TV station news and updates. I am your host Lyra McKinnon, taking you through this session. Our guest today remains Ms. Tapiwa, who is the co-author of the popular novel – Black Romance. It has really been fun, hasn't it?" Lyra beamed.

"Yes, it was really fun." Tapiwa said honestly, beaming as she stared at Lyra. If truth be told, Tapiwa didn't expect much on the first day she arrived at Jeran. But getting to know the wonderful staff, and sharing the experiences that had led her to write the book, was in fact – a blessing. It was something she would have never dreamed of a year ago. Just like every session, they began with trifle matters, and half way delve into a different chapter. As the time began to count down, the cogs of the past were in place once again.

***

Isaac was a professional gospel singer in his mid-forties. He had never been married. His reasoning was – *'Long term relationships didn't work out'*. His main job was long haul truck driving. He was always going to the United States due to work. He was also a family friend Tapiwa had never met. He was the neighbor to her great uncle. His father was a pastor, and he grew up with her family. Tapiwa felt she could trust him a little, knowing the history they both shared. But little did she know, that it would once again be an ill-fated relationship. He was living in a hotel, and said he hadn't had time to find something he liked; as he just moved from Toronto. Because of his work, he was always away. "It will be a nice break" He assured her. "Besides, you can use my hotel room." He added.

Tapiwa had never been to Montreal, and so she was excited. She arrived in Montreal late at night. As she walked through the doors of the exit pass, she spotted the man who she presumed to be Isaac. She could tell who he was from the pictures she had seen. On first sight, Tapiwa noticed one thing. He was short; slightly taller than she was. Tapiwa was not impressed with the height, but he was handsome and light skinned. His voice was crisp, and the excitement of the memories she would create in Montreal was all she could think about. They went to his hotel, and since it was late at night, Tapiwa was extremely exhausted. She couldn't think about any other thing, and went straight to bed. She felt awkward since he kept staring at her.

"You are really beautiful." He said, in one of the moments she caught him staring.

The next day, feeling more refreshed, and ready to tour, Tapiwa showed more enthusiasm than she did yesterday. Isaac showed her how he recorded his songs. She liked the fact he could sing, and she always wanted to date a musician, but not a popular one. Montreal felt like a food-cation. There were so many restaurants to choose from. Although she spent most of her time alone, since he had to go to work; eventually, he took a couple of days off, and they drove to Quebec City.

***

Tapiwa was ready to breathe in the landscape, and savor the land. The city looked like a little Paris. Although the buildings were old fashioned, it brought out the beauty and charm of the city. It had a romantic vibe to it. They went on a boat cruise around the city. Everything was going perfect. Tapiwa is someone who is big on religion, and Isaac seemed to center his conversations to belief. Days later, the mood shifted. His manager had changed his route for work. Isaac had a complete meltdown. Tapiwa had never seen anything like this. If she knew better, it was almost like he was suffering from bi-polar. One minute he was the nicest guy, and the next minute he was a complete stranger.

Having worked in mental health, Tapiwa thought she could handle it. She thought wrong. Isaac's behavior was like a keg of explosives. He was doing too much too soon. Tapiwa had not built a solid foundation with him, and had not decided if she really wanted to be with him. He continuously had tantrums, and Tapiwa was always subjected to being the listening ear, and defend him. It was draining. She didn't feel like she was with a partner, she felt like she was his therapist – an unpaid one at that. She didn't have problem listening to his troubles, but it was what all their conversations were centered on.

A month later, Tapiwa was sick. The feeling of nausea, dizziness, and an indigestion that would never go away. She knew this feeling all too well. She was pregnant. She could not imagine dealing with his mental health, and having his child. By the time she broke the news to him. He was ecstatic. He had one child prior to their relationship, and his daughter's mother would not allow him to see her.

Tapiwa felt chills run down her spine as he said his next words. "I knew the condoms had expired, so I always had the hope that it would work." He laughed. Tapiwa felt the hairs on her arm rise in fear and anger. It was intentional. She was torn. As the days went by, she felt more conflicted. The next day, while she was on the phone with him, her roommate's brother came downstairs to do laundry. Hearing the sound of a male at the background, Isaac said. "That must be the baby's father." He laughed. It was only her rommate's brother doing laundry downstairs. It was only the beginning of the long strings of insinuations and assumptions. He would often say comments like 'he was not the father of the child.'

He made Tapiwa so guilty for wanting an abortion, emotionally blackmailing her with words like "It's a sin. It is hell-worthy." He also made promises of moving her to Montreal in the summer, and also paying her dowry. Distraught, Tapiwa confided in one of her girlfriends. Hearing both sides, her girlfriend warned her about how everything was so rushed. He was hiding his mental health. Everything seemed so fast, and Tapiwa felt dizzy most times. She was never given an opportunity to think and decided her next step, Isaac made sure of that. In the blink of an eye, Tapiwa was looking at houses in Quebec. It was going to be hard for her as it was a French-speaking province.

All the stories he told her about his child's mother began to make sense to Tapiwa. The poor woman probably went through an emotional rollercoaster with him. The pregnancy was extremely hard just like the first one. Tapiwa could hardly eat anything. Tapiwa told him she would keep the baby. She was thirty-two, and it seemed like the right age. Isaac did not care about the fact that she was still legally married. He wanted to pay for her divorce. In her heart, and in her dreams, Tapiwa knew the baby was not meant to be.

Alone, and staring at the picture of the ultrasound, the sounds around the hospital ward began to drown out. Tapiwa could not see or hear anything. Her attention was focused on the child she was never meant to have. She began to envision a future with the kid, and every single scene ended up disaster. She knew she could not do this to the little child that had no sin. She could not do this to the innocent child. She stared at the ultrasound one more time, and kissed it. "I am sorry baby." She said, a sob escaping through her lightly parted lip. A tear rolled down her cheek as she tried to hold on to her emotions. "Mommy can't have you right now, please forgive me." She sobbed. She clutched the picture to her chest for a long time; barely aware of the time that had passed. Hours later, Tapiwa finally gave in. She called the Women's clinic, and booked an appointment to have an abortion. Be it fate, or a twisted kismet, there was a free appointment on that same day.

Steeling her nerves, Tapiwa took a cab to Edmonton. The driver kept getting lost, and doubts began to linger on her mind. She began to wonder if this was a sign from God; a sign for her to keep her baby. Eventually, she got to the clinic and filled out her information. There were a lot of women present, and Tapiwa was mildly surprised. All of them looked like they were deep in thought. As the proceedings went, Tapiwa had to meet a counselor first.

The faint smell of antiseptic filled the air, and Tapiwa could feel her palm get sweaty as she sat down in front of the counselor. The first words she said broke down the walls Tapiwa was trying so hard to hold on to. "It must have been hard." She said.

Tapiwa tried so hard to withhold her tears, but she could feel her lips quiver, and her nail bite deep into her palm as she tightened her fist. She wanted nothing more than to forget about the moment, and go home. She thought of all the things Isaac would say, and how difficult it would be; especially the fact that she was half way through her nursing program. Tapiwa felt like she had no control of her world. She was no longer the driver of her own life, and she was constantly swayed by emotions that never lasted long. *How did I let this happen?* She wondered, biting hard on her lower lip.

She got some medication to calm her down, and also for pain. Tapiwa looked at her baby for the last time on the ultrasound monitor, tears rolling down her cheek freely. Her throat burned from stifling the sounds of her sobs, her eyes felt gritty, and she could feel the beginnings of a headache. "Mommy is so sorry" She said repeatedly as she rubbed her belly. Tapiwa began to feel really drowsy, all she could remember was the flashing lights as she was wheeled into the operating room. The doctor asked if she wanted to see the remains, Tapiwa couldn't bear to – she said no. She passed out through the entire procedure, and by the time she was well awake, she was rolled out, and asked to seat on a recliner. By the time she woke up, she didn't feel any better. She felt terrible, and wished she was numb to the pain that ripped her apart.

Although she felt terrible, the blossoming feeling of new hope pushed its way through. It felt like a rebirth. She remembered the emotional damage it had done to women she knew, some would cry for days. For her, it was the opposite. As she walked out of the building, she felt so enlightened. She was once again, in control of her world. Tapiwa didn't feel sick anymore, and as three days rolled by, she decided it was time to tell Isaac. She thought she would feel nervous as she heard his voice flittering through the speakers. But she didn't. She felt strengthened by an invisible pair of hands that was lightly pushing her from behind. "I got an abortion." She said calmly.

Just like she had imagined, he was in disbelief. But Tapiwa didn't have the time to humor him any longer.

"Forget about me. Forget about me moving there." She said. He went on many tantrums, and called her a murderer. But he had no hold on Tapiwa anymore. His words stung, but it did not stab through her unbreakable will. As the days went by, he would send her gifts, apologizing. Fed up, Tapiwa eventually moved, and Isaac did not know where to send his gifts. He wanted a fresh start with her. Tapiwa knew what it was all about. The nature of his job didn't give Isaac access to meet up with ladies; he also could not speak French.

To finally close that chapter of her life, Tapiwa decided to go back to Montreal. They drove to the United States border. Tapiwa was going to be his ride along. She was told she could not go because she was not an essential worker. Isaac had the worst mental meltdown she had seen so far. He started shouting, and swearing at the border officer; he was out of control. He was like a bulldog barking away. Tapiwa could not believe this was happening, and she did not want to be a part of it.

As they turned around to drive back to Montreal, it was filled with six hours of nonstop shouting. Tapiwa wasn't sure how she got herself into that position. Keeping silent, and trying her hardest not to react to his insults; Isaac kept trying to get a reaction. They were on the road, and Tapiwa kept thinking of leaving at the next stop. But then again, her clothes. As an alternative, she kept quiet; and at that moment, Tapiwa knew she was finally done with him.

She did feel bad for him, but she could not keep pouring into an empty cup. She was not the one for him, neither was she a therapist. He needed to seek medical help. Tapiwa was also drained. She was not completely healed from the abortion. When she got back to his place, she packed all her clothes, including what she had left before. She was not coming back. He refused to take her to airport, and Tapiwa realized that perhaps it was better. This way, she didn't have to endure the ride to the airport. She ended up calling an Uber, and although he tried to block her way, she finally got out. Tapiwa almost missed her flight, and couldn't help but curse the day she had met him. She regretted coming back for a closure that she should have ended on the phone. But this was it – there was no going back.

From that point forward, Tapiwa was just done with dating. The urge, the sentiments, they were all gone. She didn't feel the desire to be intimate with anyone. Her past had left her scarred and traumatized. Although she looked fine from the outside, her past relationships had left a number. And worst of all, she would forever remember that her mistakes and decisions had made her terminate a life. Tapiwa swore at that moment, that as long as she lived, she was not terminating another pregnancy.

Dealing with aggressive people in the past was very difficult for her. She never saw her father raise his voice, everything seemed perfect. She thought marriage was so blissful. Looking at her extended family, they also seemed so happy; and Tapiwa thought she would meet the same type of person, soft in nature, a provider and a leader. After her relationship with Isaac, Tapiwa was left to mourn her old self; a being who tolerated a lot. She also had to discard the expectations she had as a little girl. She was in charge of her happiness again, and the best lessons she learnt were from actual experiences, on the *training ground*.

Chapter Twelve

NEW BEGINNINGS

Nate and Tapiwa kept in touch when she left Tulum. He stayed for a couple of extra days, and although she thought of extending her ticket, it was too expensive. Tapiwa was holding on to the hope that the energy they felt in a foreign land would not die down.

It didn't.

They talked about meeting again. But Tapiwa knew she couldn't afford to travel for a while since the Tulum trip was rather expensive. She had gone beyond her budget, and it would take a while before she had the means to travel once more. Tapiwa was not sure if the feelings were mutual. The courtship process of Africans was rather aggressive. While being courted, the female would wake up to wonderful messages, poems etc. Nate on the other hand, is laid back. His style was something she was not used to. And despite their difference in culture, he intrigued Tapiwa. She couldn't help but ask why he was so cold. She understood his reasoning, his background and past experiences. He described it as a seed, and if she kept giving it sunlight, and feeding it; it would eventually sprout. The old her would have stopped texting because of pride. But what she felt was a love she had never felt before.

With Nate it was different. The emotions she thought she had once lost were back in full force. Tapiwa felt like a little girl. She felt the sweet nothings of a first love, naïve and absolutely pure. She could not stop caring about him. Over time, their efforts began to pay off, and Tapiwa couldn't help but notice that Nate had improved. He was giving back the same energy she put in. They were both trying their hardest, and the miles that stood in their way felt incomparable to the happiness they shared.

As such joy continued to build up, Tapiwa would often find herself awake at night; staring at the ceiling, and grinning for no reason. She wasn't mad, she wasn't going insane. She was just deep in throes of joy. On a whim, she randomly got a ticket to Atlanta. Although it was only a month since they had last seen each other, Tapiwa missed him so much. She missed being able to reach out and grab his hand. She missed seeing his face, she missed being in his warm embrace. They had never been intimate. They had only a shared a kiss, and Tapiwa could differentiate the feelings of infatuation to what she felt at that moment. It was a fervor she knew wouldn't go down unless she saw him. They had both discussed meeting in about four months, but Tapiwa knew she couldn't hold on till then.

She had a sudden thought. 'What if the fire burns out as we both get busy?' After all, they were both busy people, with tight schedules. It wasn't the first time a relationship had dwindled that way, and eventually – all communication stops. Tapiwa wanted to make sure that she was making the right decision. Repressing those thoughts, she focused her energy to a long-term relationship. The sudden urge to confirm the strong emotion she was feeling filled her mind and thoughts; and Tapiwa knew. She knew she would be sure after the trip. As the days grew closer, Tapiwa grew anxious. *'Am I really going to Atlanta?'* She wondered. Nate had mentioned that she would meet some of his family members, friends and maybe his daughter. There was so much to think about. She wondered if she was blind to a lot of things. After all, feelings made people overlook a lot of red flags. But there was one way she could detect such warnings, and that was through his family. It is the close family and friends that identifies these warning signs.

Most importantly, Tapiwa was worried about the cultural difference. She had spoken to her aunt about her visit, and she said "You need to show respect to everyone in his family. You need to kneel to greet them'. In Tapiwa's culture, there is a certain way a prospective meets their partner's family. It is with the utmost respect. They have to be very humble, and dress very conservative. For women, they dressed in a very long dress or skirt, and for men they usually wear formal clothes. Usually the boyfriend does not meet the family, unless he is ready to make marriage arrangements. Those cultural differences made her worried. But that was not all. She was also plagued by the thought of meeting Nate outside Mexico; in his comfort zone.

Tapiwa hoped it would not be awkward. She had heard about Atlanta when she was in her teenage years. Watching music videos, and movies were the only inkling she had with Atlanta. Tapiwa kept imagining Ciara in a song with 50 cent, with an opening scene starting off with the lyrics 'It is very hot in Atlanta'. Therefore, her idea of Atlanta was a lot of buildings similar to New York, very hot, with a lot of black people.

In past years, she had heard about Atlanta being very good for black businesses. That was inspiring. Tapiwa also wanted to see what people like herself were doing in Atlanta. She also heard Tyler Perry opened his own studio. What a story! From homelessness to actually having his own production company. She knew coming to Atlanta would motivate her. But even though she was overwhelmed with curiosity, Tapiwa didn't think she could see herself staying there, because she was very comfortable in her county; back in Alberta. Tapiwa was just recovering from a cold when it was time to fly to Atlanta. Her heart was pounding while she went for a COVID test. 'Negative!' the result read, but the urge to check once more; just to make sure it was truly negative, made her go for another test. In the end, it turned out great. After that, there were no other hurdles.

Tapiwa flew from Edmonton, stopped in Calgary, and then Atlanta. Nate had traveled to Boston, and so Tapiwa was going to get to his house before him. The airport was huge, and simply chaotic. She regretted packing a lot of clothes as she dragged her luggage behind. Looking up at that moment, Tapiwa caught sight of the arrival sign. It had peaches on it saying – 'welcome to Atlanta.' Besides her motherland, Tapiwa had never seen so many black people in an airport. It almost felt as if she had boarded the wrong plane, and she was back in Zimbabwe. All she wanted to do was sit there, and stare at the people that walked by – the hairstyles, the fashion, and the attitude. Back in Canada, it was scarce to see such a large crowd of black people, and so it was a nice change. Tapiwa got an Uber, and headed to Nate's house. During their journey, the driver chatted away about hockey in Canada. But Tapiwa's attention was outside.

From the airport, she mostly saw vegetation, trees and plants. It was not how she pictured Atlanta, and it reminded her of Mexico.

She liked it already. It seemed spacious, and full of land. Nate arrived later in the evening, and Tapiwa couldn't describe the amount of happiness she felt at that moment. They went to get Chick-fil-A. She was shy at first, but Tapiwa felt really comfortable by the end of the night. Nate got her a Boston sweater from his trip. That day, they spent the rest of the night watching TV and cuddling. The next day, they went downtown Atlanta. They had talked about gritz, and Tapiwa was excited to have her first gritz experience. Tapiwa had no idea what it was. She always thought it was cheese, but instead it looked like cornmeal porridge.

Back in Zimbabwe, there was something similar they ate, while adding peanut butter, sugar, butter and milk. She gave in to her inquisitiveness, and blended it with other food like eggs, bacon, waffles. It tasted really good.

Downtown Atlanta was beautiful. It was filled with so much graffiti art. Tapiwa could also spot people selling water on the road. It reminded her of how it was back home. Out of all the places Tapiwa had visited in America, Atlanta felt closest to her motherland. They took a walk downtown, and she was happy to see African clothing stores. There were so many different stores. Nate said to her "You will find your tribe, you will find your people in Atlanta; for example black people who like rock and roll." He summed it up well. What Tapiwa saw was opportunity. There are so many ways of making money. When Tapiwa saw a man selling his smoothie from a cooler, putting in consideration the heat plus, the smoothies looked really colorful and cool. The hustle was certainly real.

One thing she did observe in difference to Canada was how people in Atlanta were reserved. Back in Canadians mostly greet each other, even as strangers. And as the saying goes, Canadians are known for smiling, and are much more approachable. There were a few friendly people who were easy to converse with. They ended the day doing a nature walk. It was the side of Atlanta Tapiwa really liked. There were so many trails and parks, complemented by good weather. Some neighborhoods had clubs that had gyms, pools and tennis courts. This is something Tapiwa hardly saw in Canada. All they had were just a few really rich neighborhoods.

While walking by a small river, Tapiwa's feet became incredibly itchy. "The mosquitoes in Atlanta are surely aggressive!" She said to Nate, half joking as she scratched a spot. The itching became unbearable, and Tapiwa had no choice but to remove her shoes. Freaked out, Tapiwa spotted many ants on her feet. Nate told her that they were fire ants. This was Tapiwa's first fire ant experience. They certainly set your skin on fire, but pouring water on her feet helped to relieve the burning sensation.

The following two days Tapiwa followed Nate to his jobs. She was able to see a side of him, she admired. He was a serious professional, and she watched as he put his all into his work. She could not help admiring the fact that he had a good schedule, and did what he loved, while working for himself. Nate and Tapiwa were very much alike in that aspect. She hated having a full time job because she loved to travel, and take breaks when she wanted to. They were driving down as he was leaving a voicemail it sunk in. Tapiwa was really dating a black American. Nate had a great figure of speech, and he is articulate with his words. She fell in love with the depth of his voice; it was so soothing. Having visited the USA, Tapiwa struggled with understanding accents. But with Nate, Tapiwa was really surprised to understand everything he said.

He took her to a flea market. It was very similar to the flea markets in Zimbabwe. The only difference was a sign at the entrance that indicated no guns allowed. That was a friendly reminder to where Tapiwa was. During her visit, she did not see anything out of the ordinary, not even a gun. But she couldn't dispel such fear. It was one of her fears about living in America – gun violence. Where she came from, people in physical fights used their fists instead, and it was usually the last resort. It was usually soldiers or police with guns. Canada on the other hand hardly had gun violence. There were many hair spots in the flea market, and all the hairdressers were from Africa. Most were from West African.

They went to a jewelry shop inside the flea market. Her attention quickly went to a couple who looked young, probably in their early twenties. The young man was helping his lady put a diamond necklace on. It felt like a scene from a music video, and Tapiwa couldn't help but think that it was so romantic, while her heart melted with joy. She thought Nate was getting himself some jewelry, but instead - he surprised her with a silver necklace, with an alphabet of his family name. Tapiwa was in disbelief, shocked and so thankful. She gave him a big hug, and kissed him. Although it wasn't the first time he got her jewelry; that moment held so much meaning.

Back in Tulum, while Nate was helping her put on an African necklace, it broke. They had passed through a jewelry store, where he had purchased a necklace, with a very nice black stone chain. Nate liked stones, and their meanings and strengths. He picked out a yellow necklace with a matching bracelet and bought it for her. No one had ever done this for Tapiwa. He was naturally a giver, and Tapiwa liked that about him.

They went to the Stone Mountain afterwards, a famous hiking mountain surrounding Atlanta. Climbing up the view was so serene. They took pictures. The mountain had a lot of stone. It was a painful climb to the top. Tapiwa wanted to give up, but Nate kept encouraging her, and told her the view at the top was worth it. They finally made it to the top just in time for the sun to set. From the top, Tapiwa could see most of Atlanta was forest. It was dark when they made their way back. Not letting go for a second, Tapiwa held Nate's hand. She could barely see anything, and it reminded her of the time they went up his attic. She was afraid of heights, and Nate had told her to hold on to his hand. The only reason Tapiwa went there was because, going up an attic was on her bucket list. She had never been in one, and in Canada she was only used to basements. Nate's reassurance made her feel safe, and their foundation had a great start already. Tapiwa knew she wanted to hold his hand through this journey called life.

By the time they reached the bottom of the mountain, it was really dark. It was around 10 pm. The gates were now closed. They walked through a dark forest to reach another gate; it was really scary. So much for being adventurous. As they reached the gate it was also locked. There were two options: either jump, or turn back and walk through the dark forest again to find another entrance. Tapiwa could not imagine jumping over the gate. The last time she had done something like that was in kindergarten. Tapiwa could not see herself finding other entrances either, their only solution was to jump. Tapiwa did not have such courage, and she could feel her legs tremble. Nate explained how to do it, and followed with jumping over; to show her how to navigate over the fence. Tapiwa climbed up and reached the top, looked over and froze.

There were cars passing at the bottom, and the gate was by a bridge. One wrong move and she was done for. She slowly climbed down, and felt a huge relief almost immediately. She was still weak in the knees, and could only watch as Nate did his climb effortlessly. Looking back to that moment, Tapiwa could only laugh. It wasn't fancy, but it had turned to a core moment. On their way back to Nate's house, they met a couple that complimented them. Tapiwa couldn't help but smile. Once again, she could feel her heart beating fast.

The next day, they went to the Atlanta Botanical Gardens downtown. It was a Saturday and many people were there. Nate and Tapiwa spent most of their day there. It was magical. A little haven, filled with hundreds of plants species. They used a map as a guide around the garden. They also found a plant with Nate's family name. Tapiwa thought that was amazing; to find a plant with the same name as you, was pretty cool to her. It did not matter where they went, as long as Nate was there, they had a good time. Together, they created so many memories. The next day, they headed to Macon; which was over an hour drive from Atlanta. It was a small town where they met his friend who was renovating his house. They later had dinner. Tapiwa liked the small city better, since traffic was not her favorite part of big cities. This was the night before Tapiwa had to fly back to Canada. Tapiwa thoroughly enjoyed her stay, and was sad that she was leaving already. That night, she met Nate's daughter, aunt and cousin. It went better than expected. They were all really nice to her, and Tapiwa enjoyed getting to know them. Nate introduced her to one of his close friends, and to his friend's sister who were both in real estate. They were all business oriented. Nate certainly had good people around him, which was important.

While counting down to go back to Atlanta in just over three weeks, Tapiwa knew the time would come when Nate would meet her family in another state, in another country. During the time she was with him, she enjoyed quality time the most with Nate. She loved cuddling, playing board games, and she could tell that what they felt wasn't tied to Mexico. The connection was real and natural. It was now official. She really did not have a straight explanation of why she came to Atlanta, but Tapiwa got all the answers. She needed and wanted them to work out. Of course, their journey would not be perfect. They still had a lot of differences, but that was the beauty of it. Tapiwa was loving the experience already, and there was so much to learn about him and his culture. An example was how dowry is paid with cows. Him being open to her culture was admirable. They had been transparent with each other, and they tried to keep it that way. Respect and trust are important, and Tapiwa couldn't help but think that it has contributed to how they flowed. But they have yet to overcome conflicts that would come in the way. Tapiwa wasn't sure where she heard it from, but the sentence explained how important it was to know someone in all their seasons. A season of happiness, sadness, wealth, broke days, and also testing out how you could live together. Change is both exciting and scary. For Tapiwa, moving to Atlanta to be with Nate would be a future plan. The plus side was business opportunities, and a lot of entertainment, big airport and black empowerment. The weather was also great, and there were lots of trees and plants similar to the time Tapiwa lived in Zimbabwe.

When Tapiwa was in her last year of high school, she once had a choice for university between Canada, USA and Australia. Tapiwa had chosen Canada mostly because it is known to be quiet, and safe. She didn't choose Australia because of her fear of snakes and poisonous spiders. It also didn't help that she had heard many horror stories.

Are they rushing things? This thought occasionally occurs. She was sure they both knew what they wanted. They had both grown and learnt from the past. It was time for both of them to be happy. Tapiwa knew they would both take their time, and do what was needed correctly. Like Naomi said to Ruth in the bible "For wherever you go, I will go. And wherever you live, I will live, your people will be my people."

Tapiwa believed life is not meant to be lived in one place. And going forward, they would move in love, transparency, and respect. Tapiwa was glad she had met Nate. It happened so unexpectedly, but she no longer felt like she was on this journey alone. To new beginnings!" Tapiwa read out loud. As she looked up, she realized this was it. This was really the end of the interview. She could see their eager expression, and she knew they wished she could continue. "The last full stop might be present, but our journey is only beginning." Another encore erupted.

Made in the USA
Columbia, SC
01 September 2022

65734120R00069